Ricki Cliff
On Her Own

by

Gregory Brazzil

Life to Legacy, LLC

Ricki Cliff: On Her Own
by Gregory Brazzil Copyright © 2025

ISBN 978-1-947288-83-6

Printed in the United States
10 9 8 7 6 5 4 3 2 1

Cover Design and interior layout by
Legacy Designs Inc.
Legacydesigninc@gmail.com

Published by:
Life To Legacy, LLC
P.O. Box 1239
Matteson, IL 60443
www.Life2Legacy.com
708-272-4444

TABLE OF CONTENTS

A WORD FROM THE AUTHOR

The creation of Detective Ricki Cliff was a challenge that I created for myself. I wanted to step into the shoes of a female law enforcement officer who works the streets of a big city, such as Chicago. For decades, we've been bombarded by characters portraying male police officers on the meanest streets of our nation. Additionally, Hollywood's portrayal of a female police officer often depicts someone who appears to be a supermodel by day and a Dirty Harry figure by night. My goal was to change that image. Ricki Cliff not only allowed me to portray a woman's point of view on crime, but it also enabled me to reflect on the real-world situations that law enforcement professionals face on a daily basis. Through it all, I must admit that I had my share of fun with the Ricki Cliff character by making her a rebel with a sharp edge. If you enjoy *Ricki Cliff: On Her Own*, you'll be pleased to know that this novel is the first in a series I'm creating, featuring this character.

—Gregory Brazzil

INTRODUCTION:

My name is Ricki Cliff, and my peers refer to me as a motorcycle riding, red-headed lesbo, with a bad attitude toward men. The word around the office is that I'm bad news to work with, and apparently, that word has sunken into the adolescent skulls of the brass! Need I say, that they're of the male persuasion? Not even my female co-workers, are willing to ride shotgun with me. Yes, I break some rules. And yes, I crack a few heads unnecessarily, but that doesn't make me the horrible person that I'm seen as around the office. At this point, if you're a normal human being, you're probably wondering what kind of work I do, and where the hell do I work at!

Well, the answer is, I'm a detective with the Chicago Police Department, and despite my "shiny" reputation, I'm known for getting the job done. I admit that working alone comes with pros and cons. One of the pros, is having the brass take my word over a piece of street scum, who I accidentally broke the wrist of, during arrest. One of the cons is when I've chased some punk into an alley and suddenly find bullets coming in my direction from behind me when I have no partner, to back me up. It is what it is.

Despite it all, I love my job. When my dad was alive, he was a cop, and it wasn't ever my intention to follow in his footsteps, and yet, here I am. I spend my days and some nights, playing cat and mouse with some of the worse human beings that nature has so graciously given us. Some crimes are just crimes, but then, there are the ones that truly get under my skin, and that's when I become the bitch that my peers see me as.

A couple of the crimes that I hate, are people that use other people to stake their claim. Another, is the adult scum who take advantage of kids for their own personal gain. Generally, money or power is the common denominator. With those combined, they easily build a Fortune 500 company for themselves. To be honest with you, I could care less about what the I.R.S. thinks of these people, but when the tools of their trade, include the trafficking of young girls, and leaving behind a string of dead bodies, that's where I come in. I don't get them all, but I feel like I'm making a difference.

At the end of my day, I go home to a dark apartment, and cold pots. You shouldn't be too surprised to learn, that I'm a loner. I don't even have a cat, but I manage to be happy. I consider a good day, locking up some scum, taking a shower, and reclining in my Lazy Boy with a shot of Jack and a cold beer. If I'm lucky, I can catch The Late Show before it goes off. Come along with me, as I lead you through my next investigation.

1

JUST ANOTHER DAY

It was a Tuesday morning and I was still in bed, after a night of staking out an abandoned apartment building, A.K.A., crack head flop house. It turned out to be a total bust, but when you're a narc in a city the size of Chicago, you have to follow every hunch that you get. As I sit up in bed, I can smell coffee brewing. I'd forgotten that I'd set the timer before passing out last night. I stood up rubbing that crap out of my eyes and opened the blinds, giving me a view of the park, down below my 9th floor apartment window.

In my tiny kitchen, I poured myself a mug of joe and looked inside the refrigerator. I never learned to cook. I guess that I'm not that kind of girl. This morning's breakfast is a buffet of assorted carry-out items, most of which, is beginning to develop a life of their own. I settled for a leftover slice of Gino's pizza.

I sat my coffee down on the end table and sat my ass down in an old brown leather Lazy Boy recliner, that I inherited from my Pop. It was the only thing that I took from his house, when he died. Using the remote, I turned on my flat screen TV, the only appliance in my place that was made within the last ten years. It looks like I dropped in about half way through the morning news cast. Great! On the screen, was that damn Candee Harris, with W.L.O.K., sticking her nose in our business again! I swear that I can't stand the chick, but I have to admit that she's a real hottie. I have mixed feelings about men and women, and have never allowed women to peak, my curiosity, but at the same time, I have my thoughts about her. It seems, that these damn reporters have nothing better to do, then blow our leads! It's a wonder that we solve any cases at all. Miss Harris, herself, is actually one of the city's most popular news anchors, and she's seen nightly on TV, by millions, which doesn't make our job any easier.

As I sat yelling at the TV, I finished my breakfast of the champions, and headed for the shower. While waiting for the water to get hot, I stood before my full length mirror, observing my nude body. I couldn't help but notice the fruits of my labor. On my left thigh is a scar left from a bullet that I caught. On my right shoulder I could see where another one passed through. I smiled at myself thinking, that if nothing else, I'd make a great poster child for what not to do, for a living.

I had to drag my butt into the shower, but once that I was in, I didn't want to get out. I slipped on a pair of spandex shorts and an old sleeveless sweat shirt. I put my red hair into a ponytail and took another look at myself in the mirror. Not bad for an old chick, if you call 42, old. Speaking of age, I've found that keeping a regular workout routine, aids me in keeping up with the bad guys. My first stop this morning, is the precinct work-out room. It's not like a big health club, but it has the basics to keep a body in shape. I grabbed my gym bag from the closet and started packing my basic necessities. Some toiletries, a pair of jeans, an old blazer that I like, pepper spray, a pair of handcuffs, and my Glock. Yeah I know, not your typical gym bag goodies, but I am who I am.

I grabbed my helmet and headed out the door. My main method of transportation is a fifteen year old Harley Sportster. It's old, but it's my prize procession. The department prefers that I drive one of their Victoria's. They're great in the fall and winter, but they stick out, like a sore thumb.

I'm the only woman on my squad, and that puts two points against me. For starters, I get the bottom of the barrel, crap cases, that none of the men want. My second problem is, bringing in perks that have unexplainable injuries. Unfortunately, being a woman doesn't give me the luxury of letting a two-hundred pound man strike me first. Needless to say, none of the good ole' boys are willing to partner up with me, and that's just fine.

I strapped my gym bag to the rear of the seat, on my bike and fired my baby up. I hopped on and pulled off, quickly. On some occasions, the rumble of my bike sets off car alarms in my building's parking garage.

That pisses off the neighbors, so I try to make a speedy exit. The ride over to the precinct was nice. For this short period of time, I feel like a normal citizen.

When I pulled into the department's parking lot, I passed by two female officers. They didn't know it, but I could see in my mirror that they were laughing and pointing at me. You would think that we women could come together and support each other, especially seeing that most of the male officers think that we're not capable, of doing the job. It really pissed me off!

I parked, took off my helmet, grabbed my gear, and went inside. The first officer that I saw was the only man with the department, that I respect. He's the desk sergeant, Sergeant Brown to be exact. He's a big husky man, that's counting down to his retirement. Rumor is, that he was once one hell of a cop, on the streets. He's seen a lot of changes in the department, most of all, he's seen promotions pass by him. When I stepped into the lobby, he looked down at me over the counter, like a judge at a hearing.

"Good morning Detective Cliff. How's my princess, today?"

"Morning Sergeant. Are ya holding down the fort?"

"I'm doing my best, but of course, that's a matter of opinion!"

"You're preaching to the choir now, Sergeant."

"You know, the captain's going to love that outfit that you have on!"

"Yeah, I know. I'm trying to make a beeline to the workout room, right now, and between me and you, the captain can bite me!"

"Have a good one, Ricki."

When I walked into the workout room, a couple of male officers were already getting their exercise in, and when I bent over to put my gym bag down, the adolescent behavior started. The two officers began cat calling and whistling at my ass. Now, the typical female officer would have gone straight to H.R. and filed a sexual harassment case, but when it comes to dealing with children, I like to handle my own matters. Instead of filing a complaint, I decided to squash their precious, little male egos.

"You two guys need to grow something bigger than a cocktail weenie, before you pucker up to whistle at my ass!"

One of the officers dropped his weights immediately, and jumped in my face. Lucky for him, his buddy grabbed him by the shoulders and pulled him back, because I had my hand on the can of pepper spray, in my gym bag.

"Come on, man, let's get out of here, and leave this cold-hearted bitch, alone!"

"Bye, bye boys!"

It's been a while since I've had to put a couple of these so-called men in their place, but I admit that it felt good! I got my workout in and headed for the showers, making sure that I locked the door behind me.

2

THE PEANUT GALLERY

After workout and shower I changed into a more suitable outfit, for a plain clothes officer. It wasn't time for me to clock-in, but I figured that as long as I was at the precinct, I may as well stop at my desk and see if anything new, had landed on it.

It's always interesting coming in unannounced, on a different shift. Even though my badge is displayed, I still get strange looks, from strange faces. I like to give people the benefit of the doubt, and just assume that they're curious. I carried myself like I normally do, and just as I was sitting down, at my desk, I was approached by a male officer.

"Hi, I'm Detective Winston, and let me guess, you're Detective Cliff."

"So I take it that you've heard of me."

"You bet ya, honey!"

"So what's that supposed to mean?"

"Oh nothing, just a buddy of mine that works graveyard, mentioned you a time, or two."

I was thinking that this guy is a real Bozo, and then he goes and proves it, by turning around and giving the other officers a big shit eating grin.

"If you don't mind, I'm kinda busy here, Detective Wilson."

"That's Winston."

"Whatever!"

I know that the pricks that I work with, act childish during our shift, and that's one thing, but when they start spreading rumors about me, around the station, it's another. The sad part is, that half of them, are married, and the other half are losers! They all want to get in my pants, but sense I treat them like a bunch of retards, they spread rumors that I'm a dyke. The truth is, that they don't know a damn thing about my personal life!

After refocusing on my original mission, I noticed that a case had indeed landed on my desk. Attached to the front of the file folder was a Post-it note that read, priority. See me first thing. It was signed by Captain Keller. When I opened the file, the first thing that I saw was a photo of a beautiful young girl with brunette hair. She looked to be about sixteen years old. Before reading any further, I got a big knot in my stomach. I feared turning the page, because it reminded me of my own kid sister, that I lost to drugs on the streets of this city.

I took a deep breath and turned the page. My biggest fear came true. Not only did this kid have a history with Crystal Meth, but she's run away from home. She was last seen in the company of a pimp/drug dealer. I immediately closed the file folder, because I didn't want to see anymore. I unlocked the cabinet next to my desk, put the file away, locked the cabinet and took off. I needed to clear my head, so that I could act like a professional later tonight, when I meet with the Captain. As hard as I try not to, I take kid cases personal. It's only 11:00am right now, and I have plenty of time to get my act together.

A BLAST FROM THE PAST

Just as I sat on my bike my cellphone vibrated. The name that I saw on the screen was an old friend, that likes to live on the edge, from time to time. He shows me a good time and I keep my mouth closed. He's not married, but he's a City Councilman, that has a very bright political future. Even though he knows that there are people out there, that would love to catch him with his pants down, he still likes to hook up from time to time.

"Well, well, well, if it's not Councilman Lee! To what do I owe the pleasure?"

"Put any bad guys away, lately?"

"Define bad guys! Do you mean bad guys, or bad guys like you?"

"I feel like stepping out of the box today. I'm down at the harbor. Why don't you join me, for lunch?"

"So, Mr. Councilman, you're in the mood for taking risk! What the hell, I need to clear my mind anyway. I'll see you in a little bit."

CLICK.

Councilman Lee always have been fun, to hang out with. It's a shame that he's built a career around himself, that won't let him enjoy the basic needs of life. It's even worse that he has to sneak around, to spend a little time with someone like me, a person that's not acceptable in his circle. I don't know if it says something about me, or the wealthy women in his world. In any case, a great lunch onboard his boat, out on Lake Michigan, sounds good right about now.

I put my helmet on and headed for Lake Shore Drive. Once that I'd reached the lake front, the drive was wonderful! I wanted to keep on driving and ride away from this whole stinking life! The problem is, that I care about people, too much. Even though I'm enjoying the ride, and about to have a little mid-day pleasure, I can't get this kid off of my mind. I haven't even started working on her case, and it's making me crazy.

Once that I was able to see the harbor, off in the distance, my mind began shifting gears. I was now making the mental transition from this kid to Councilman Lee, jeopardizing his political future. It's not that having my name next to his, on the front page wouldn't bother me, but I'd rather not deal with it. I have no choice, but tell him that this will be our last little get together. I can just imagine the crap that I'd have to go through with the jerks at the precinct, if they got wind of us.

I parked my bike and started walking down the boardwalk. It wasn't long before I saw the councilman's craft. I call it a craft, because it's too big to call a boat, and too small, to call a yacht. All that I can say is, politics have been very good to him! Still standing, on the boardwalk, I called out his name. He immediately came up from the galley with two glasses and a bottle of wine in his hands.

"Welcome aboard, matey!"

I smiled and climbed onboard. I could tell that he was ready to attack me, right then and there. He handed me the bottle and glasses, and without a word, he untied us from the pier, and fired up the two big engines. Moments later, we pulled off and headed out on Lake Michigan. When we got to where the city looked like a miniature village, he cut the engines and dropped anchor.

As he poured wine, I took off my blazer, revealing my pistol and cuffs. We both sipped from our glasses and he looked behind me, at my cuffs.

"So, tell me Detective. Do you plan on putting those things on me?"

"No, not unless you want me to!"

He put his arms around me and began kissing me on my neck.

"There's something that we need to talk about."

"Ah, come on, Ricki! Stop worrying! We're way out here in the middle of nowhere!"

"Aren't you the least bit concerned, about your future?"

"Of course, I am, but can't we at least enjoy the moment, while we have it?"

"OK, have it your way, but we still need to talk before we head back. Now, take off that shirt!"

"I will, if you will!"

So I did.

3

THE DEVIL'S WORKSHOP

In a rundown motel, in the Englewood area, on the south side, sits three people. On a lumpy bed, sitting nervously, is a grossly overweight, balding, pathetic man. Rubbing his hands, he waits and watches. Sitting on a filthy sofa, is a muscular Black guy, in his forties. His head is shaved clean and he has tattoos as far as you can see. He's holding a lit disposable lighter, at the end of a glass pipe, that has the opposite end, between the lips of a young girl. As she inhales from the pipe, she drifts further and further away from reality. The Black guy then looks over at the John, sitting on the bed, and smiles.

"It won't be long now, my man!"

Another fifteen minutes goes by, he stands and walks over to the John. He then sticks out his hand and is given a roll of bills.

"I'll be back in one hour, have fun!"

Before leaving, he helps the young girl, over to the bed and lets her fall on it, like a rag doll. Upon leaving, he failed to realize that he left the pipe and more crystal meth on the table, in front of the sofa.

After thirty minutes or so, of what he thought was going to be a good time, the John sat up and took a bottle of whiskey from his jacket pocket. He drank half of it and threw the open bottle on the sofa. He then got on his feet and stumbled out the door, leaving the girl behind.

It was difficult, but she crawled over to the cocktail table. Through trial and error, she managed to reload the pipe, but the challenge, was lighting it. She kept dropping the pipe, and finally in a fit of rage, she threw the pipe and the lit lighter on the sofa, and fell over sideways to the floor.

Time went by.

Outside the motel, a crowd was gathering, and off in the distance, you could hear the sound of fire engines getting closer. All of this happened as Councilman Lee and I, floated on Lake Michigan, having an afternoon romp. I had no idea.

4

WHERE THE HELL, ARE YOU?———

O n the way back to the harbor, the councilman and I finally had the talk, that I'd been waiting to have. We went around and around. After a while, I started believing that he got off on living on the edge, just as much as he did on me. We agreed to cut things off, for a while. As we pulled into the harbor, I still didn't believe that he'd keep his word, and avoid contacting me.

He and I said our goodbyes and stepped off the craft. Just for the hell of it, I checked my cellphone, for messages. I guess that the signal wasn't too hot, out there on the water, because I had four messages from my captain. I wondered why he'd be calling me, during my time off, and why was he on duty, for that matter? With each message, I could hear his temper getting higher and higher. In his last message, he was screaming!

"Where the hell, are you?"

I hopped on my bike and high tailed it home. I couldn't go in this way. I had to shower and change clothes. After I had did all of that, I sat down and called the Captain.

"Where the hell, have you been, Ricki?"

Before I could answer him, he cut me off.

"Get in here, A.S.A.P.!"

CLICK.

For him to be calling me during my time off, meant that something bad had gone down, and I was preparing myself for the worst. I grabbed my helmet and headed for the precinct. When I arrived at the station and walked into the lobby, the sergeant, gave me a funny look.

"I don't know what you did Ricki, but the Captain's been screaming out your name!"

"Jesus, I'm not even on duty, yet!"

"Well, just tuck and roll, Ricki!"

When I reached the squad room, the captain was standing in the doorway, of his office.

"Do you want to grab the file that I left on your desk, and join me in my office, Detective?"

I didn't say a word. I just went to my desk and removed the file from the cabinet. I then turned around and walked straight into his office, and closed the door behind me.

"Have a seat, Detective. Look, I know that you're not on duty yet, but I needed you yesterday!"

"What the hell's going on, Captain?"

"Let me have that file."

He opened it and turned it around, so that I could see the young girl's face. He then tapped the photo with his forefinger.

"Terri Wallace, is in a burn unit, hanging on by a thin thread!"

"What happen to her?"

"A fire broke out at a sleazy motel in Englewood, and the firemen found her inside. They're doing mop-up right now, and I'm waiting to hear from the Battalion Chief, to find out how it started, but I do have my suspicions."

"Why do you say that?"

"It's not the burns that have her hanging on by a thread, it's the amount of crystal, found in her body."

"Jesus Christ, Captain!"

"You'd better get over there, why you can, and get as much as you can! This kid, might not make it!"

This was a time when I ignored policy, and took my bike, instead of an unmarked squad. Unless some moron, opens a car door in front of me, I'll make far better time. I have to admit, that a siren and lights would've come in handy. I parked near the hospital's emergency entrance and ran straight in to the nurse's station, flashing my badge.

"This is an emergency! I need to see Terri Wallace, a burn victim, brought in earlier."

The nurse, sitting at the desk, got on the phone right away.

"Doctor, she's here... okay."

She hung up the phone

"The doctor's coming down, and he wants to talk to you on your way up."

"Thank you."

After a five-minute wait, I saw the doors to the elevator open at the end of the hall. A gentleman, wearing a lab coat with a full head of gray hair, stepped out. He approached me and I extended my hand.

"Good afternoon Detective, I'm Doctor Liptoll. Please, come with me."

"Tell me Doctor, what are her chances?"

"It's a little too soon, to say for sure, but I've seen kids come in here like this before, and I have to say, that things don't look good for her, I'm sorry."

"Do you think that she'll be able to understand me?"

"She's in a daze, but I'm sure that she'll be able to hear you."

Just as we were about to step out of the elevator, the doctor told me that Terri's parents were sitting in the waiting room. I stepped out thinking, damn! I hate this part of the job. First things first, for now,

I'll talk to the kid, while I can.

Every time that I find myself in the I.C.U., I get the same feeling. It's a feeling of sitting in death's waiting room. It's not that everyone here is going to die, but it gives me a creepy feeling, that closure is right around the corner. In Terri's room now, the doctor pulled back the curtain, and I braced myself for what I was about to see. Aside from the usual scent of antibiotic ointments, the kid's arms, face, and head were wrapped in bandages. There was an IV in each hand and two machines monitoring her. Through an opening in the bandages around her head, I could see her eyes, peering out at us.

"Detective Cliff, I'm going to leave you two alone, for now."

As he turned to leave, I stopped him.

"Doctor, there's one more thing."

The Doctor immediately, cut me off.

"No, she wasn't. There were signs of recent activity, but not forced. If you need me, I'll be right outside."

I wanted to rest my hand on her arm in an affectionate way, but I didn't know if it would hurt her. I got as close to the bed, as I could.

"I'm Detective Cliff, and I'd like to ask you a few questions, if you don't mind. You don't have to speak. I'm going to place my hand near yours, and if it's OK for me to ask you questions, I want you to touch me."

Slowly and gently I put my hand near hers. It took a few moments, but she lightly touched my hand.

"Honey, touch my hand again, if you know what happened to you, today."

First, she turned her head away, and then, turned her eyes back, towards me, but didn't touch me. God, this poor thing! She doesn't even know about the fire.

"Was anyone else, there?"

At first, she stared at me a long time, and then she turned her head away, again. I waited a moment and then asked again. Finally, she looked at me and I could see that her eyes were red, from tears, and that gave me my answer.

"Was it a man, honey?"

It was obvious, that this kid was terrified of something, or someone. Suddenly, she surprised me, by touching my hand.

"What is his name, honey?"

She paused for a moment, and then for the first time, I saw her lips move, but I couldn't make out what she was saying. I leaned over her, held my hair back and put my ear close to her mouth. There was a faint whisper, but I thought that she said the letters, TJ. I stood straight up and she turned her head again. I felt that I'd pushed her enough, for one day, and decided to leave.

"Thank you. Get some rest for now. I'll come back tomorrow, to see how you're doing."

It took all that I had, but I put on the biggest smile that I could, and said goodbye. I turned around to leave, thinking that I knew two things about this kid. I knew that she had sexual intercourse, and there's someone out there with the initials TJ, that's involved. Aside from seeing this kid like this, the number one thing that pisses me off, is the fact that some no-good bastard, left her to die!

My intentions were to check on the parents and try to give them some ray of hope, but I detoured to talk to the doctor again. He was standing behind the counter, at the nurse's station.

"Yes, Detective."

"Doctor, you said that she had had recent intercourse."

"Yes, according to the exam that she was given."

"Were any fluids, other than her own, found that will provide a DNA simple?"

"I'd have to check with doctor that performed her exam, and she won't be available until tomorrow."

I reached into my pocket and took out one of my cards.

"Can you have her give me a call, please?"

"Sure, Detective."

I sat at a small round table with Terri's parents, and right away, I noticed that I wasn't the first cop that they'd discussed their daughter with. I could also see, that raising a child like Terri, had taken toll on them. They admitted that they'd lost her trust and respect, a long time ago. They didn't know why. All that they'd done, was to love her and give her the best that they could. I hated to ask them, but I had to know if the letters TJ, meant anything to them. They both, immediately, looked at each other. Mr. Wallace stood up and rubbed his face.

"The last time that we saw her, we had one of our big knockout arguments. The last thing that she said before storming out, was that we'd never understand her, and only TJ cares about her. I tried to ask her who this TJ person was, but she took off. We reported her missing, and now we're here with you."

"Does she have any friends, that you know of?"

"Do you mean, normal kids, that do homework, or go to football games on Friday night, and eat junk at sleepovers?"

I had no answer for Mr. Wallace, and his wife burst out in tears. God, I could feel their pain! I touched both their hands with mine and placed one of my cards on the table. I then left the waiting room.

5

DOWNTIME ———————

I knew that I wasn't going to get much done, tonight, so I went in to give the captain an update and requested daytime hours for tomorrow. He'd spoken to the Battalion Chief, and he'd come to the conclusion that the fire started with alcohol spilled from a whiskey bottle, found on the sofa. It was accompanied by a lighter and a glass pipe that shattered from the intense heat.

I asked the captain if he could spare one of the lab boys, tomorrow. He said yes, but doubted that I'd find anything of use. Before leaving, I asked if the entire motel room, had been destroyed.

"It's funny, that you should ask that. According to the fire fighters, the bathroom door was closed during the fire. The outside of the walls and door was charred, but the inside was hardly damaged."

"Well Captain, I've got something cooking, and if I get lucky tomorrow, we may have us a pretty good lead."

I was drained by all that had happened at the hospital, and I couldn't sleep. I couldn't help but compare this kid to my own kid sister, and everywhere that I looked, I saw the faces of Terri's parents. I finally gave in to the idea, of going out for a drink. A few years back, I met a nice group of people, when I donated a blood sample at a drive, that was held at a Hyde Park bar. I'd told one of the owners, that I'd come in some night, and tonight's that night.

I got myself together and moments later, I was pressing the starter button on my Sportster. It was a beautiful night, as I headed south on Lake Shore Drive. To my right was the glow of the city, and to my left stars hung out over the lake. I got so caught up in the view, that I missed my turnoff, and ended up getting off L.S.D. near the museum.

I drove past the front of the bar and went around to the parking lot, where there was a side entrance. After parking my bike, the first thing that I noticed, was this bad-ass sixty something Corvette! It was silver and white with red leather interior, and the top was down. After drooling over it a moment, I went inside.

I've always been the kind of girl that's confident and secure, so I had no problem bellying up to the bar. I put my helmet on one stool, and put my ass on another. This great looking, Italian guy, that I remembered from the blood drive, walked up and greeted me.

"Welcome to the City Block. My name is Louie. What will be your pleasure?"

"Now honey, let's not talk about that! I'll take a double Jack and a Bud on the side."

"Sounds like you had a long one!"

"Honey, you have no idea!"

It was a weeknight and the place was about half full, which was fine with me. Usually, in a case like this, it's the regulars that keep the fire burning. It wasn't long before Louie returned with my drinks.

"Here you are, my dear."

"By the way, I'm Ricki."

"I'm pleased to meet you, Ricki. This Bud's on me."

"Well, that's awful sweet of you!"

"Around here, we like to see new faces, become regular faces."

"Tell me Louie, who owns that Corvette, outside?"

He pointed to the other side of the room.

"The guy over there with the lady, owns it."

"I've seen that woman somewhere, before. She's very pretty!"

"She's a model. Maybe you've seen her in advertisements."

Louie moved along and I devoured my drink. I decided to go for a second round. Being a cop, I couldn't keep my nose in my own business. As I drank, I observed the crowd. I noticed a couple coming in through the same entrance that I'd used. The woman was an attractive young Asian woman, and the guy smelled of cop! I was thinking that there must be something special, about this guy. Usually, cops date other cops or lawyers. The daily filth that they work in changes them morally, and they understand each other in ways that other people can't. Don't get me wrong, I'm no prize either, but I call 'em the way that I see'em.

With no one really to talk to, I began watching a pre-recorded broadcast of this evening's news, on a flat-screen TV, mounted on the wall. The sound was muted, but the picture being shown was definitely my motel and my fire. Footage of the paramedics rolling someone away on a gurney was shown. The good thing is, that I now have more than just a mental picture of the scene.

Even though I'm sitting here drinking, I'm planning tomorrow's agenda. I don't know why, but the initials TJ, were bugging me. Maybe I can go through our computer files on known pimps and the A.K.A. that they use on the street. If I'm lucky, maybe this guy will have a sheet somewhere.

Just as I was about to call it a night, Mr. Cop stepped up, to order cocktails. I was shocked when he spoke to me.

"Good evening, officer."

"Excuse me!"

"I'm Detective Little, with the 33, and you're Detective who?"

I smiled and said, Detective Cliff.

"I guess that we can say that this is a small world, Detective Cliff."

"How did you know, that I'm a cop?"

"Well, you're drinking alone. You're having a Cop Special, which is a shot of whiskey with a beer back, you're checking everyone out, and I can see that Glock under your jacket."

"Man! And you call me a cop!"

We toasted and he walked away with a smile. I left that night thinking that was a cute incident.

6

THE SLEAZY MOTEL

Morning came and I headed straight for the computer on my desk. I pulled up records on known pimps, pushers, and petty criminals. I typed in the letters TJ under the A.K.A. column. These files consist of hundreds, if not thousands of names. I decided to let my computer do its thing, and I took off for the motel in Englewood, to meet with the lab guy.

When I arrived, he wasn't there yet and the place was still taped off. The front wall of the room was completely gone, except for enough charred 2 by 4 framing members that were supporting what was left, of the roof. I got a bad feeling about stepping into the place, so I contacted the Battalion Chief, to make sure that it was safe. He said that it was safe, but he stressed caution. Just as I hung up, the lab guy arrived. We introduced ourselves and stood looking at the place, for a moment.

Damn, another intercity business shot to hell, said the lab guy!

"The owner may get a check from the insurance company, but only a fool, would rebuild in an area like this."

"Yeah well, this place wasn't exactly the Embassy Suites!"

"So, what are we looking for, Detective?"

"Come with me and let me show you something, that you're not going to believe."

Stepping carefully, I led him to the bathroom, where we both stood staring, because, we were a bit blown away. Aside from some smoke stains on the walls, the John was spotless. I slipped on a pair of latex gloves and began pointing out the areas that I was interested in. While he was doing his thing, I stepped back into the main room. I stood in the middle trying to visualize the scene, as it played out. I picked up a stick that looked like it may've been part of the back of a chair. Using it, I began poking through the ashes. I really didn't know what I was looking for, but my mind told me to do it.

Under the edge of the bed, on the floor, I saw a small corner of a piece of foil. Using the stick, I pulled it out. Lo and behold, it was a condom package. This could be the needle in the haystack, that I was hoping for. I waited for the lab tech to finish in the bathroom and join me.

"Did you find anything, useful?"

"I lifted some partial prints off the doorknob, but that's about it."

I pointed at the foil with my stick.

"Do you mind, bagging that?"

Before leaving, we both looked around, but there was nothing of any value that hadn't been destroyed by fire. I knew that this lab tech had plenty of cases in his lab, but I had no choice, but to ask him to put a rush on it. He said that he'd do his best to get back to me, A.S.A.P.

I drove back to the station, to see if my computer had come up with anything. Walking up to my desk, I could see that it had stopped running, and the monitor had fallen to sleep. I moved the mouse a couple of inches to the side, and bang, there it was. I'd gotten a hit.

In the upper left-hand corner, there was a mug shot. Another photo showed this guy's right shoulder, which had a tattoo of a skull with a snake coming out of one of the eye sockets. The funny part was, that the letters TJ, stood for Thaddeus James. No wonder he goes by TJ. His last name is Clemons.

I began reading and found that Mr. TJ has been a thorn in the public's ass since he was thirteen and busted for shoplifting in a dime store. His entire life has consisted of drug use, possession with intent to sale, battery, assault with a deadly weapon, pimping, and extortion. For some reason, he's never done a long stretch. Personally, I'd like to shut him, just for the hell of it, both him and the lawyers that kept his ass on the streets.

This guy has all the makings of a nut that avoids prison, until the day he goes ape shit and kills a room full of people! Normally, that's when the media gets a hold of it, and make us cops look like a bunch of freaking idiots!

Even if Terri survives, from my experience, she'll never testify against this jerk! Even worse, I'd hate to see the look on her parent's face, when they find out about TJ's record. At this point, all that I can do is attempt catching him in the act, with another unaged girl. I've seen enough of this crap, for now! It's starting to make my stomach turn.

I made a printout of what I found on Mr. TJ, put it in a new file folder, and locked it in my file cabinet. Minutes later, I was on my bike enroute to the hospital. My main objective was to pay my new friend a visit, as I promised yesterday. That's to be followed by a conversation with the doctor, that examined her. I'm praying that she found useful DNA.

Once again, I took a deep breath, before stepping into this kid's room. To my surprise, she was sitting up in bed, indicating that she was slowly recovering. I stood in the doorway and said Hi.

"Do you remember me, honey?"

Just like before, she turned and looked away before answering me.

"Yeah, I remember you, so what!"

"I guess that you're doing better. Perhaps, this is the real you! If we're being ourselves, why don't we cut through the BS! Why don't you tell me about Thaddeus James?"

By the sudden movement, that she made, I could tell that I'd shocked her. Some of the bandages had been removed, revealing some facial expressions. It was a shame that her lovely face now had burn damage.

"So, tell me about TJ. How did you meet him? What does he mean, to you?"

"He means everything to me, if you must know!"

"Why were you at that motel?"

"That's none of your business!"

"Do you love him? Do you think that he loves you? I hope that you don't love him, because he left you in a burning building, to die."

"You're wrong, he wouldn't do that!"

"Let me make sure, that I've got this right. You're in love with a guy that helps you nearly overdose on crystal meth, and leaves you in a burning building, just to save his own ass!"

It was obvious, that this kid was too far, gone, and wasn't going to volunteer to work with me.

"Alright, honey, let's try a different approach. Do you love your parents?"

"I don't have any parents!"

"There are two people in the waiting room, that love you dearly, and they're worried sick about you."

"That's not true! All that they worry about is themselves!"

When she said that, my first thought, was to slap her ass into next week! I was already the enemy, and that wouldn't help things.

"Well, tell me honey, do you remember anything at all, about the motel?"

"Don't you have something else to do? Because you're wasting your time here."

"You said that TJ would never do something like this, to you. Assuming that that's true, who were you there with?"

"That's none of your business!"

"So, you do remember being there!"

"So, what if I do?"

"Look kid, you can hate me, and you can hate your parents, but hating yourself is just freaking stupid! I know that there was someone else there with you."

"You're wrong! I was alone."

"Is that what TJ trains all of his girls to say?"

"Go to hell!"

"So, you want me to believe that you rented that room, yourself?"

"Yeah, that's right, I did it myself."

"Well, that's good. Now, all that I have to do, is check the motel registry. Tell me something else, Terri. Do you make it a habit of checking into motels, just to get high and set yourself on fire?"

"Why does it matter, to you?"

"Honestly, it doesn't matter to me whether you like setting yourself on fire, but I'm a cop and my job is to find the jerk that did this to you. And I have to try to keep your ass alive at the same time! If it's all the same to you, I'd appreciate it, if you stopped screwing around with me!"

I must've struck a nerve because she started crying. Who knows whether or not the tears were fake, but they were tears all the same.

"Look honey, I don't want to do this the hard way, but I will, if you give me no other choice. It's obvious that you're confused about what love really is, and you've worked yourself into a very dangerous corner, that you can't get out of. If you want my help, I can get you out of this mess. I can make sure that TJ never lays his hands, or eyes, on you again. We can make your body healthy again, and you can go back to doing the fun things, that girls your age, are supposed to do. On the other hand, the doctor that examined you, has a DNA sample from the guy that was there with you. Once I let him sit his ass behind bars for a while, I'm sure he's going to trade TJ for his own ass, which will make TJ think that you betrayed him. Right now, I'm going to meet with that doctor, find out who owns the DNA sample, and then I'm going after that guy. In the meantime, you can lay here and decide what you want to do with the rest of your life."

I left Terri's room, knowing that I'd sold her a bill of goods, but it wasn't all lies, plus I did what I had to do. The truth is, that she's no different than any other teenage girl, that thinks that she's in love. The problem is that they tend to give new meaning to stupid! That's when someone like me, steps in and slaps them back into reality. Hopefully, with a little luck and a lot of prayers, I'll be able to save this kid from herself.

Finally, I spoke with the doctor that examined Terri, and she had indeed found enough male pubic hair, to produce a DNA sample. I was so happy that I could have hugged her, but I had to put myself in check; because I knew this sample wouldn't place the owner in the motel room. Any rookie Public Defender would say that this guy was just another one of Terri's Johns. I guess that the doctor's news, was the little bit of luck that I was talking about. Now, if my prayers get answered, my lab tech will have good news for me.

I had done all I could at the hospital, so I packed it up and headed back to the precinct. The first thing that I did, was shoot Captain Keller an email, and bring him up to date on what I've found so far. The red light flashed on my desk phone. I found that my lab tech had left me a message, and wanted me to contact him A.S.A.P. I wasted no time in returning his call.

MY FAVORITE LAB TECH

When I dialed his number, I reached the equivalent of a receptionist answering the phone at the lab. I was placed on hold and waited for what seemed like forever! Finally, he answered.

"Detective Cliff, I'm sorry for keeping you waiting for so long."

"That's alright! Tell me, what do you have for me?"

"Well, I didn't get any DNA off of that foil wrapper, but I did get a partial right-hand thumb and index finger from the door knob."

"That's great!"

"Hold on, not so fast, Detective. I ran what I got against the prints on the computer files, and only got a few points on each print. But this information and something that I saw yesterday at the motel encouraged me to return to the scene. There was a whiskey bottle with a little fluid in it, lying on the floor."

"The Battalion Chief said that the fire was likely fueled by whiskey from that bottle."

"Yes, I know, and when we were there, I thought that the fluid in the bottle was water from the fireman's hose. When I returned to the scene, I discovered that the fluid in the bottle was actually a swallow of whiskey. Now comes the good part; it had saliva mixed in with it."

"You're kidding me!"

"It gets better. There was enough to get a DNA sample."

"Well, I'll be damned! This has been one hell of a day!"

"It sounds like you got a hit on your end, too."

"I did, and if our samples match, this DNA is going to blow this case wide open."

"Let's get together, first thing tomorrow morning, Detective."

"That works for me!"

CLICK.

I spent the rest of my day trying to run down cops that had busted TJ in the past. As it turns out, two of the arresting officers had retired, and one was no longer with us. I left messages with three others. I was trying to get the heads up on some of TJ's habits and possible hangouts. I don't expect him to show up at the hospital, with flowers and chocolate! That means that I'm going to have to find him and shadow his activities. Maybe, he'll lead me to some of his other illegal endeavors.

I know that Terri's afraid to testify against him, but she may be willing to tell me where he hangs out. Tomorrow I'll take another crack at her. I knew that it was a reach, but I decided to run a DMV check, to see if Mr. TJ has a vehicle registered in his name. It didn't take long, and I was blown away by what I saw on my monitor! This son of a bitch, that's never worked a day in his miserable life, or paid a freaking dime in taxes, has not only a Benz registered in his name, but a Harley Fat Boy! Who the hell says crime doesn't pay!

Just for the hell of it, I'm going to see if this jerk has a mortgage, and if he does, I'm going to sick the I.R.S. on his ass, so that they can take all his toys away. That little venture is going to take some time, so, for now, I'm going to call it a day.

7

BUSTED!

Stretched out on my recliner, I'm enjoying a nice frosty cold one. While the TV set watches me, I continue to dwell on this case. It dawned on me that I'd become completely obsessed with this TJ jerk. Every time that someone like him walks out of a courtroom, a free man, they become more and more arrogant. At some point, they begin to think that they're untouchable.

If TJ was a skilled safe cracker or had the brains to engineer a major bank job, I'd have a little respect for him. The fact that his criminal success is based on manipulating teenage girls, or worse, a weak substance addict, shows just how small he really is. I can already tell, that if I don't nail this bastard soon, he's going to eat me up from the inside out.

After a couple of cold ones, I dozed off. At around half past 6:00pm, I was awakened by a police-style pounding at my door. While reaching for my sidearm, I was wondering how anyone, got up to my floor. At the same time, I got a shock that I prayed, that I'd never see. In living color, on my flat screen TV, was Councilman Lee and me in his craft, on the lake. Both of us, with a wine glass in our hand, him with his shirt off, and me without my shirt, but the media was kind enough, to place a black strip across my boobs.

HOLY MOLEY!

The pounding on my door wouldn't stop. With my pistol pointed straight out, I snatched the door open. To my surprise, it was Captain Keller, and he blew past me, like I didn't even have my gun drawn.

That's when the yelling started!

"Ricki, I've seen you do some stupid things, and Lord knows that I've been to the ends of the world to save your freaking badge, but this takes the damn cake! What in the hell, were you two thinking? No, please, don't answer that! I've always known that the councilman was an arrogant son of a bitch, but Jesus, Ricki, didn't you know that you were playing Leap Frog with a damn elephant? You've really done it, this time!"

Just as I was about to try and get a word in edgewise, the captain grabbed me by the arm and pulled me over to the window. I took one look out the window and damn near passed out!

"Jesus Christ!"

"Jesus Christ, is right! Do you know who that is, out there?"

"Yes Captain, I know."

"Well, I'm going to tell you anyway! That woman out there, is the biggest motor mouth, and pain in the ass, that the department has ever had! She's going to have the city as a main entrée, and your ass, not mine, is going to be the cherry on top!"

Everything that the captain said was true; I had really screwed up this time, and seeing Candee Harris with her W.L.O.K. News Crew outside, proved it. Finally, my apartment got quiet. I fell back in my recliner, and the captain helped himself to a beer from my refrigerator. I hadn't noticed, but my cellphone had been vibrating repeatedly. Both of us realized it at the same time, and when I reached for it, the captain snatched it out of my hand.

"Give me that! This is just great!"

He showed me the name of the screen.

"Do you see the prefix, after the area code?"

"Yes Captain, I see it."

"How would you like to bet your career, that it's the councilman on the other end?"

I turned my back and looked out the window again.

"Yeah, that's what I thought!"

He then opened my refrigerator again.

"Do you have any scotch, around this place?"

"There's a bottle of Jack in the cabinet, above the refrigerator."

He took two glasses out, poured himself a shot, and downed it. He then poured us both one and handed me mine. Man, did I need it! Once again, my place got quiet, except for my cellphone vibrating.

"Either answer that damn thing or turn it off!"

I opted to turn it off, and that's when I decided to face the music.

"So, what now, Captain?"

"Well, for starters Ricki, don't talk to the councilman. I'm sure that everything on the air or in a wire is being recorded. By the way, you need to stay here until you hear from me. Your friend, the councilman, seems to enjoy controversy, and he's a true politician. He'll find a way to cover his ass! You on the other hand, are a horse of a different color. At this point, all that we can do, is work on damage control."

The captain got up to leave, and I stopped him at the door.

"Thank you, Captain."

"Don't think for one damn second, that I'm finished with your ass!"

With that, he left, slamming the door behind himself.

8

ON LOCKDOWN

I stood at my window, watching Miss Harris doing her on the spot coverage, and I'm sure that her network wasn't the only one out there. There had to be other reporters waiting for me to step out, so that they could feast on my limbs! Off in the distance, I could hear multiple rumbling noises, getting closer. Moments later, a small group of Harleys came cruising down the street, drowning out all transmissions that the reporters were attempting to broadcast. I loved it. I felt like they were here just for me. I wish that I could've hopped on my bike and join them.

It was that very same interruption that reminded me of Terri's case and my meeting tomorrow morning, with the lab tech. The problem is, how can I do it, if I'm locked up, here? I can't let this case sit idle, and I knew that the captain couldn't be back in his office yet, so I took the opportunity to leave him a voice message.

I went to my door and looked through the peephole. The hallway appeared to be clear, so I eased my door open and dashed across the hall and knocked on my neighbor's door. She opened the door right away and had a million questions. I told her that I didn't have the liberty to talk right now, but I could really use her phone. I reached the captain's desk phone and left him the details. After that, I returned to my apartment and waited for the next bomb, to drop!

It was after 10:00pm when my cellphone vibrated. I rolled over in bed to read the name on the screen. It was an unknown number that left me a voice mail. On the other end, I heard a male voice.

THIS IS DETECTIVE LITTLE, RETURNING YOUR CALL REGARDING A HOODLUM BY THE NAME OF TJ.

I had forgotten all about the calls that I'd made earlier, before all this mess started. I wrote the detective's number down. Earlier when I was going through TJ's past arrest records at my desk, it didn't occur to me that Detective Little, as listed on the file, was the same guy I met at the Hyde Park bar. I was glad that he returned my call, but his timing sucked.

I paced around my place, going over everything, and then it hit me; Detective Little could be some help to me, after all. I went back across the hall to my neighbor's place and begged to use her phone again. I called the detective and he answered right away.

"Detective Cliff, I got your message earlier. I'm sorry that it took me so long, to get back to you."

"That's OK."

"I'm sure that you know how my day, has gone."

"I'm afraid so, but I do have information on this clown, TJ!"

"I can see that he's left a bad taste in your mouth, as well!"

"Yeah, he's a piece of work, that's managed to fly under the radar for years. I first met Mr. TJ at a Vice Raid taking place at a biker bar, which was being used as a front for the human trafficking of young girls."

"You've got to be kidding me!"

"I wish that I was, but he was found to be a small fish, and booked on some misdemeanors, that he walked away from."

"Yeah, I've noticed that getting off easy, seems to be his forte."

"Is there anything else that I can do for you, Detective?"

"Well, now that you've mentioned it, I really need a big favor. As you know, I'm in quite a tight spot, and so is my ability to communicate with others. As of right now, I'm using my neighbor's phone."

"So, what is it that you need?"

"I know that I'm asking a lot, but I could really use a cheap burner phone, from a convenience store."

"No problem, but how will I get it, to you?"

"Well, my place is being watched by the media, and I'd hate to drag you into this mess. How about that Hyde Park bar, that I met you at?"

"OK, give me about an hour."

"Thank you, Detective."

"You're welcome, but call me Max."

CLICK.

I knew that I was taking a risk, but if I'm going to be stuck here, I need contact with the outside world. One way or another, I'm going to transact business as usual, right here at home. I checked the hallway again and made my way to the service elevator. When the doors opened, I found myself in the boiler room. There were multiple mechanical sounds, as well as pressure being released from a variety of valves. I turned the deadbolt on the first door that I saw, and it opened next to the dumpsters.

When I left the garage on my bike, I was surprised to see that the media gang had given up. Some of these guys will stop at nothing, so if someone was there, they were hiding. As long as I wasn't being approached, it was fine with me. I had a date to keep, and that's what I was focused on.

I arrived at the bar in less than an hour, a little early. Detective Little, or should I say, Max, wasn't there yet. My helmet and I both, took a seat at the bar. I was expecting to see the handsome Italian guy behind the bar, but in his place, was the lovely Asian woman that I saw with Max, the first night, that I came in.

She was warm, bubbly, and polite. She reminded me of myself, before I took the oath. She was everything that a woman should be. As for me,

43

I spend my days with the world's parasites! I can't remember the last time, that I had my nails done, or have some guy send me flowers, for no reason at all. To quote a new friend, this seems like a good time for a Cop Special!

I was halfway through my beer when Max took a seat next to me. He slid the phone to me under the bar. At the same time, the lovely young bartender leaned over the bar and kissed him, another thing to make me green.

"Thanks Max, this means a lot to me."

"You're welcome."

"As long as we're going to be on first name basis, I'm Ricki."

"Wait a minute! You're Ricki Cliff?"

"Oh God, no, please don't tell me that you've been drawn into the rumors!"

"Relax, I'm not a member of that club, but I have heard your name mentioned in some major cases."

"I should've known that you were on the up and up, when you didn't ask me about the councilman."

"Look Ricki, I'm easy going, but if you want to talk about that, I'll listen."

"You know Max, I think that we're going to get along just fine."

9

A LONG NIGHT

I made it back home before midnight and took the same route through my building, back to my apartment. I immediately started charging my new phone. I was really tempted to contact Councilman Lee, but I had already disobeyed one of the captain's orders just hours after he left.

During the night, I rolled from one side of the bed to the other. A little bit of everything went through my mind, as you can imagine. Stuff like, TJ, being caught in a raid at a biker bar, and the fact that he currently owns a Harley. There was also the way that Terri reacted, when I asked if TJ trained all his girls to behave the way she did. It was obviously, that a trickle of jealousy, was in her veins. I've got to find a way to talk to her again.

She can't be the only girl in TJ's stable. The one thing that I can do, is squeeze the hell out of whoever owns that DNA sample. I think that TJ is too smart for it to belong to him, however, he had to have set some guy up with Terri, and something went wrong. If I'm lucky, the guy's done business with him before, and if I'm really lucky, it was with a different girl.

I had pushed myself as far as I could on this case. I'd finally hit a wall and gave it a rest. I puffed up my pillows and found a good spot on my bed, but still had problems falling to sleep. The only remaining subject on my mind, was what the headlines would say in the morning. I can see it now.

CITY COUNCILMAN RISKS IT ALL WITH ONE OF CHICAGO'S FINEST!

I can see two photos below the headline. One of which, would be that of Councilman Lee, and the other one would be the two of us, half nude. I'd really like to blame him and be pissed off, but the truth is, that we both screwed up. I know that I had the best intentions, when I saw him last, but it was too little, too late. Even though I'm not in love with the guy, I still feel sorry for him. He had a very bright political future. Me on the other hand, I've gone as high up the ladder as I'll ever go. I've pretty much burned all the bridges that I could get my hands on.

The most that will happen to me, is that I'll get humiliated, and put on timeout, so to speak. The good thing is, that I don't have a family that'll be embarrassed. All I really want, is to be allowed to continue working Terri's case.

If I get parked at my desk, I'd be happy to know that someone is diligently trying to nail TJ to the wall. They'd need enough hard-core evidence, so that no lawyer can get him off as usual. I want his ass in the general population, with the word of what he does to young girls, spread throughout the cell blocks.

As uncomfortable as it's going to be, I can't wait to talk to the captain, in the morning. Despite what he thinks of me, I know how he feels about Terri's case, and I'm sure that he's getting some heat from the brass. It will be great if he lets me orchestrate things from my desk. For starters, I'm the only one that has any kind of relationship with Terri, and if she's going to talk to anyone, it's going to me. Only time will tell.

10

FACING THE MUSIC

Morning came, and the first thing that I did, was look out the window. It appeared that the local networks had called off their dogs. I turned on the TV to find a completely different attitude. All the major networks were running the story on Councilman Lee and me. Some of these anchor personalities, really take the cake! It amazes me how one photograph can produce so many different stories. One station even had an interview with a political science professor, from a nearby university. He was giving his spin on the councilman's future career.

I guess that in this city, it pays to be nobody. I continued watching the coverage for about, forty minutes. During that time, I went from being pissed off, to laughing my ass off! It appears that reporters have a lot more fun doing their job, than I do.

I sat around waiting to hear from somebody, anybody. Finally, my phone rang once and stopped. I thought that it was Councilman Lee, and he had second thoughts and hung up. When I looked at the small screen on my phone, I saw the captain's number. Maybe he was trying to send me a signal. I unplugged my new phone and gave him a call, he answered on the first ring.

"Good morning, Captain."

"It's not that damn good, and where the hell, are you calling from?"

"I'm at home, and I'm using a burner."

"How the hell, did you get that?"

"Captain, sir, do you really want to know?"

"Yeah, you're right, I don't!"

"No offense Captain, but I need to know if I'm going to be on lockdown, in my apartment."

"Well Ricki, for right now, I'm waiting to hear from upstairs, so you'll have to stay put for the time being. What can you tell me, about these DNA samples?"

"The doctor who handled the rape kit for Terri, found enough male pubic hair to produce a DNA sample, and our lab tech found a sample at the scene as well. He and I were scheduled to get together this morning to verify that they match."

"What was your next move, if they did match?"

"With a little luck, maybe this scum bag has a sheet, and we'll haul his ass in for questioning."

"I'll tell you what I'm going to do, Ricki. For now, I'm going to put somebody else on it, and if this clown has a sheet, I'll have him brought in. Maybe, let you sit in during the interrogation."

"I'd love that Captain, and in the meantime, I'm going to take advantage of this phone. I need to follow up on some information that I received on this guy TJ, who's in this mess up to his neck!"

"Where did you get this information?"

"I spoke with a Detective Maxwell Little, over at the 33."

"Yeah, I know 'em, he's a good cop."

"He told me that TJ was caught up in a raid at a biker bar, a while back. It turned out, that the bar was a front for the human trafficking of young girls."

"Jesus, Ricki! I pray that there's no connection with this kid, Terri."

"I hate to tell you Captain, but Terri thinks that she's in love with this jerk, not to mention, that he has a Harley motorcycle registered to his name."

"Are you saying that these guys, may be back in business?"

"That's a possibility, sir."

"Well, see what you can find out, and please, don't make another move without telling me, first!"

"OK Captain."

"Hey Ricki, the phone was a good idea."

"Thanks Captain."

CLICK.

Well, that wasn't the best news that I've ever got, but it wasn't the worse either. Honestly, I'd rather work from home, than sit in the squad room with Larry, Moe, and Curly! I turned off the TV and turned on my computer. While it was booting up, I started a pot of coffee. Then I took a seat at my small desk, with my robe on. Not getting dressed, was another benefit of working from home.

With a mug of hot coffee in my hand, I sat in front of my computer, waiting for it to magically start talking to me. I don't have access to the department's data base, but I knew that somehow, the internet would be of value to me. I just had to find out how.

After a few minutes of losing a stare down with my monitor, I got up and walked over to my window. The activities going on across the street, at the park, has always given me inspiration. On the corner, near a bus stop, an old man was walking a small dog. He stopped in front of a newspaper machine and dropped coins inside. Just as he was lifting the front panel of the machine, it hit me!

I turned and went back to my computer. I typed in the words Chicago Tribune. Moments later, I was at their home page. In a highlighted search box, I typed in archives and pressed ENTER. From that point on, it was a game of words. In the archives, I went to police raids, which turned out to be a huge mistake. The records went back as far as Bathtub Gin and the days of Speak Easy Bars. I found myself getting nowhere fast.

It was too early in the morning for me to give up, so I typed in biker bar raids. That's when I got lucky. It was only hundreds of stories, instead of thousands. What I needed, was a specific date. At least the year would've helped. That's when I got on the horn and called up my new friend.

"Good morning, Detective Little speaking, how may I help you?"

"Good morning, Max, sorry to bother you, this is Ricki."

"Hey, I take it that the phone is working?"

"Yes, and seeing that I've been restricted to my apartment, its heaven sent! Thank you again."

"So, what can I do for you, this morning?"

"I'm trying to do some research on the internet, but I'm running into brick walls."

"What do you need?"

"I'm in the newspaper archives, looking for the story on the biker bar raid. It appears that there were quite a few of them. Maybe, you can help me out with the year that it took place."

"Hold on, while I type something."

While he did a search, I refilled coffee mug.

"OK Ricki, here we go. The year was 2007, and the month was July, July 6th to be exact, and get this, the girls were brought in on July 4th. These guys knew that the city would be complete chaos, with fireworks, block parties, parades, you name it! They had done their homework and knew that the cops would have their hands full."

"How the hell, did Vice know what they were up to?"

"They had help from a good old fashion, informant!"

"I have one more question, Max."

"Go for it."

"Did you guys ever find out how the transportation and housing of these girls was furnished?"

"Personally, I was just along for the raid. I would guess that Vice has that kind of information."

"Thanks Max, you've been a big help."

"Hey Ricki, do you mind me asking you, something?"

"Not at all, what's up?"

"How are you, holding up?"

"It's tough, but I did something stupid, and now I have to live with it!"

"Well, trust me, it'll blow over soon, and from my perspective, the focus is on him."

"Thanks for asking Max, I'll talk to you later."

CLICK.

11

BACK TO TERRI

Talking to Max was beneficial for me. Not only did he enlighten me regarding this case, but he helped me feel human again, by not judging me.

Back at my computer now, I search for headlines, published on the date that he'd given me. It turned out to be a huge story. It was big enough, to encourage some major journalist to do in depth, follow-up stories about human trafficking. Evidently, the problem is far bigger in the states, than most Americans know. For some reason, which baffles me, it's kept relatively quiet.

If TJ's job was to get these girls addicted, so that they wouldn't complain about working, then there must be 3 or 4, more powerful people above him. It seems to me, that the outfit that moves these girls, is too well organized for a street thug like TJ, to be calling the shots. For now, I'm going to concentrate on the small fish, and work my way up.

I decided to shift gears, for a moment, and reach out to Terri. I got the hospital switchboard, which connected me to the nurse's station on Terri's floor. I was in luck, because they remembered me. Due to the circumstances of Terri being there, normal incoming calls, weren't allowed.

Her phone rang three times, and I was beginning to wonder, if she was going to answer at all, but finally, she did.

"Hello, who is this?"

"Hi Terri, it's me, Detective Cliff. How are you this morning?"

"I don't know, alright, I guess. It doesn't matter, anyway!"

"Of course, it matters, honey. It matters to your parents and to me."

"Is it true, what they say?"

"What who says, honey?"

"What they say about you, on the news."

She had caught me off guard. I wasn't ready for this.

"Yes honey, it's true."

"Aren't you going to lie to me, like my parents?"

"No honey, I'm not going to lie to you at all."

"So, what's going to happen to you?"

"I don't know, but I made a stupid mistake, just like you did. But I do know that I'll be given a second chance, just like you will."

This is where I stretched the truth a little.

"You may not think so, but you and I, have something in common."

"How could that be?"

"I trusted the city councilman, just like you trusted TJ."

"But TJ loves me! Does this city guy love you?"

"Yes, but in his own way."

"What do you mean?"

"He loves me, when I do things, that he wants me to do."

This is where I really laid it on, thick!

"He hasn't called me, or come to see me, since this mess started. Has TJ called, or came to see you?"

Terri didn't answer me, but I could hear her quietly releasing tears. I think that I finally, reached her.

SILENCE.

"Terri, are you still there?"

"Yes, I'm here. Do you think that you'll ever see him, again?"

"No, honey. He really doesn't love me."

Again, there was dead silence, but this time, she hung up. I decided not to call her back. I wanted her to think about our conversation. I knew that this kid was dying for TJ to show up, like a knight in shiny armor, but even if he was allowed, it's not going to happen. I admit that I pushed her a little with my own story, but I had to let her reach that conclusion on her own. There are a lot of things that I can do for this kid, but removing the pain that she's going through, is not one of them.

The talk with Terri was mentally draining, so I decided to take a breather. It was a little past eleven, when my new phone rang, it was the captain.

"Hello."

"Detective, I just got off the horn with our lab tech, and I have good news."

"God, I sure could use some!"

"We got a hit on those samples. They were a match, and our boy has a sheet. It includes Contributing to Prostitution, Possession, and Aiding and Abetting a Minor. He sounds like a great guy!"

"So, when can we pick him up?"

"We're working on that, but first, we want to watch him for a while, and see where he leads us. By the way, he's a bartender, and we're running a make on the bar right now. Look Detective, I've got to go, but I'll be in touch with you."

Thanks Captain."

CLICK.

So far, this day has been far more productive, than I thought it would be, last night. There were still lots of work to be done, but this was a good start. As I relaxed, taking a so-called break, a new idea, popped into my head. Since I was still in the dark, about how the transportation of the girls was financed, back in 2007, I got up and returned to my computer.

A journalist that wrote a follow-up story on Human Trafficking, was a guy by the name of Robert Wilmur. I knew it was a real stretch, but I decided to contact the Tribune and see if this guy is still around. I only had one problem, and that was being able to tell him who I am. I couldn't take the chance of him having a field day at my expense, because of my current situation. If I was going to learn anything at all, from this guy, I'd have to lie to him about who I am. I hate to do it, but I need all the help that I can get.

12

TOMMY G

I managed to talk to Mr. Wilmur at the Tribune. It turned out, that I'd gotten lucky, because he was just a few months from retiring. He remembered the Vice raid and the girls very well. He informed me that these girls are brought here, from poor countries, in small groups. Usually, they're promised jobs and a better life. In some cases, the trips are even financed by the girl's families.

Most recently, they're being forced to come here, by the Cartel and gang lords who threaten the lives of their families. Mr. Wilmur hated to tell me, and I hated to hear it!

I now need to find out, rather TJ is part of a trafficking operation or just a small-time pimp. I called and left a message for the captain. I also requested two things from him. One, was the name of the bar that our suspect works at, and two, is the plate number, on TJ's bike. I know that the captain is going to wonder what I'm up to and give me a stern warning.

Part of my plan, is to find out who owns this bar, and I'm also considering taking a late-night drive, just to check out the bar's clientele. It could've been more than fifteen minutes, after I left the captain a message, that he called me back.

"Ricki, we've just got thrown a curve ball! While one of our officers in an unmarked squad was following our suspect, he witnessed a couple of uniforms on routine patrol, taking our suspect and a young Hispanic girl into custody, for soliciting."

"Damn it! You've got to be kidding me!"

"Get dressed. I'm coming to get you! We've got to roll this scum bag, right now!"

CLICK.

I hurried and got my things together. All the time, I was wondering, how the hell, he knew that I wasn't dressed. I was pleased that he was including me in on this, but riding along with him would mean, that my hands will be tied, and that may be exactly, what he wanted. I will take advantage of this opportunity, but it doesn't mean, that I'm going to change my plans for a late-night ride. I didn't know where the captain called me from, but he got to my place, awful fast! As we rode in his Crown Vic, he informed me that the suspect's name is Thomas Garner, A.K.A. Tommy G. He's currently sitting in a holding tank, until we get there.

"Ricki, you're not going to believe where the officers picked this guy up, at."

"Try me Captain, I'll believe anything!"

"While they sat parked, they watched him go into one of the rooms at the same motel where the fire broke out at. Evidently, the Fire Marshall cleared the place for operation. The officers waited fifteen minutes and then knocked on the door. That's when this non-English speaking kid, comes barreling out the door, wearing just her bra and panties. It was like fishing in a bucket, for these two cops! According to them, this motel has a reputation for low life activities. Had it not, they would have driven past it."

"Hey Captain, what do you think the chances are, that that motel is where TJ always does business at?"

"For right now, I'd say that the chances are awful damn good!"

"Do you think that Mr. Tommy G., might give him up?"

"He might, if he wants to save his own ass."

"Well, I know one thing, Captain. It's pretty obvious that Tommy G. believes that he's in the clear, regarding Terri."

"Yeah well, he's in for the shock, of his freaking life!"

"What did you find out about the bar, that he works at?"

"Oh, that place, it's a run-down dive, called Sally's, and according to my friends on the Vice Squad, it's a biker bar."

When the captain and I walked into the precinct lobby, I was immediately reminded of my little venture, with Councilman Lee. No one said anything, but all eyes were on me. The years of service that I'd put in as a good cop, didn't seem to matter. For the time being, I was the cover story of a rag magazine.

When we got upstairs, to the squad room, the looks were the same, but with humiliating verbal comments, to match. That's when the captain blew his cool!

"Alright, that's enough of that crap! The next jerk that shoots his big freaking mouth off, is going to be walking a beat for a month of Sundays! Now, get back to work, damn it!"

More than anything, I wanted to thank the captain for having my back, but seeing that I got myself into this mess, I thought that it was best, to keep my mouth closed.

13

PLEASED TO MEET YOU ———

The captain and I went to the interrogation room. Before stepping in, we observed the suspect through the one-way glass window. This overweight, bald bastard, was looking dirtier by the second, as he sat with one hand cuffed to the bolted-down table. Standing in the corner, with his arms folded, was a uniformed officer looking at him with disgust, and waiting for us to enter.

I tapped on the window, and he and I switched positions, as the captain watched from the hallway. This guy didn't deserve the normal pleasantries, so I cut through the chase.

"So, Tommy, it's good to see you again!"

He just sat, looking at me, and didn't say a word.

"Do you know why, you're here?"

Still, there was no response from him.

"Not in the mood for talking. Well, let's try a different approach. You know Tommy, you're quite a guy! It takes a special man, to have a drink of whiskey and slip on a condom, before doing a teenage girl!"

He tried to jump up, but the handcuff held him down, and the fact that I didn't flinch, pissed him off.

"Fuck you, Bitch! You don't know what you're talking about!"

"Oh, now you want to talk! As long as you're in the talking mood now, why don't you try this on for size! One count of Arson, one count of having Sex with a Minor, and one count of Attempted Manslaughter.

That's a lot of years, Tommy. Think about it, you could lose your job at the bar!"

"I want my lawyer, Bitch!"

"Oh yeah, I'm sure that they're standing in line, to represent your fat ass! If I, were you, I'd get a lawyer too. Fifteen years is definitely better than twenty-five!"

"I didn't try to kill nobody, and I don't know crap about no fire!"

"I disagree with you, Tommy. The bottle of whiskey that you had, started the fire, at that motel."

"Yeah well, that's BS!"

"Hey Tommy, guess what motel, that fire was at."

"I don't know what you're talking about!"

"OK, keep playing stupid. Lawyers love clients like you! I'm going to give you the facts, Tommy. The fire broke out at the same motel, that you were arrested at today. How should I say, in the company of a minor. You also made a huge mistake. The whiskey bottle that you left behind, had your DNA inside of it. Oh yeah, there's one other thing, I almost forgot. You left another teenage girl there, to burn to death, but you got lucky. She's in the Intensive Care Unit, where she'll be for a long time."

"I didn't start no fire, and I didn't know that she was a kid!"

"Oh, so you were there?"

I waved at the uniformed officer outside, to join us.

"This piece of filth stinks! Take his ass downstairs, lock him up, and throw away the damn key!"

That's when Tommy started pleading.

"Wait, wait, you can't do this to me! Let me say something!"

"It's too late, to talk now, Tommy! Lock this scum up!"

The officer cuffed both of Tommy's hands, behind his back and led him away. I rejoined the captain and smiled at him.

"How's that, for starters?"

The captain looked at me and then shook his head.

"No wonder, no one likes you! Good work!"

"I figure that we can let him sit in the tombs for a while, and see what he gives up."

"That's fine with me. If nothing else, we'll get him for Soliciting a Minor."

"I need a favor."

"You do good work Detective, but now isn't the time, to be asking for favors. What is it?"

"Can you give me one hour, at my desk, on the computer?"

"I guess that that won't hurt, but in exactly one hour, I'm going to have a uniform, take you home, until further notice."

I was hoping that one hour, would be enough. For starters, I was thinking, that if the motel, where Tommy was busted, was a regular spot for him, then TJ must be working with the owner, and has some kind of agreement with him.

I was a bit lost, on which state department would list the ownership of businesses, so, for the sake of time, I took a shortcut. I called the Battalion Chief, to see if he had documented that information, in his report. Unfortunately, I struck out. Feeling desperate, I sent a text message to the last person in the world, that I should be in contact with, but I knew that he could help me. That person was the one and only, Councilman Lee. My text read as follows.

BUSINESS ONLY, NO PRESSURE, PLEASE. I NEED THE OWNER'S NAME OF THE ROAD STAR MOTEL, IN ENGLEWOOD, AND SALLY'S BAR. PLEASE, TEXT ME ONLY. THIS IS RICKI.

After taking a risk, that could end my career, it dawned on me, that Max could've told me who owns the bar. I don't know why, I asked about the bar. I guess, it was just a hunch.

Next up, I called the A.D.A.'s office. I needed to know who the attorney is, that's been keeping TJ out of jail, lately. I'm thinking that his success in crime, doesn't nearly, generate enough money to keep him out of jail, for repeat offenses. He must be valuable to someone. Not only, can they afford it, but they think that he's worth it.

I was connected to A.D.A. Caplin, who was new to me, but I didn't care. After introducing myself, and giving him my badge number, I explained why I was calling, and what I needed. TJ's name didn't sound familiar to him, so he asked me to hold on, while he checked computer files. He returned to the phone and informed me that TJ's last hearing, was handled by D.A. White, who is no longer with the state, due to medical issues. He read further and came up with the name, Cynthia Lewis, of Lewis and Wilcox Attorneys at Law. I expressed my gratitude and hung up. My one hour was quickly coming to an end. As far as my text to the councilman goes, I won't know if he received it, until I get home and check my personal phone.

14

BACK ON LOCKDOWN

I could've gone further, but basically, my timing was pretty good. As soon as I hung up from the A.D.A., my desk phone rang. It was the desk sergeant, downstairs, telling me that my ride was waiting. I made my way down to the lobby, without any comments from the peanut gallery.

The quietness reminded me that the media presence at my place, had fizzled out, and I was curious about what the councilman was going through. I always knew that we were taking a risk. I only hope that the media sees it as a one-time thing, and not some flaming romance, that's been going on forever. I know that in a city this size, sooner or later, there'll be another hot topic, for the media hounds to feed on. They'll pack up their circus, move across town, and expose someone else for enjoying life.

I waved goodbye to the sergeant, and stepped out the door, to find a young female officer, behind the wheel of a squad. I introduced myself, and after some brief conversation, I learned that she had been on the force for just over three years.

"Detective Cliff, do you mind, if I ask you something?"

"I don't mind any questions that's work-related."

"How do you deal with it?"

"Deal with what, honey?"

"How do you deal with the stupidity?"

"Oh, you're talking about the male officers."

"Yeah, I mean, I expect it, out on the streets, but when I joined the force, I thought that there would be a better grade of men. I grew up with six older brothers and I'm no sissy, but I swear that there are days when I want to draw my service weapon and shut one of them in the ass!"

"Trust me, honey, I know how you feel, and the worst part is, that there's nothing that you can do about it. Knowing that they'll never have this, is what gets me through the day, and I can tell you, that they do want you! That's what makes them act like, jerks."

I gestured toward my body, as I spoke.

"Thanks, for letting me vent, Detective Cliff."

"Just keep doing good work, and when the detective exams are given, score high. The more rank you get, the less likely, that they'll be willing to risk their careers."

"There's one more thing. I was given your address, but I'm not very familiar with the community."

"You're doing fine, honey. I'll guide you when we get closer."

When we reached my place, I thanked her, wished her good luck, and told her to keep her head up. Inside my apartment now, the first thing that I did was check my phone, for a message from the councilman. One step into my bedroom, and there on the nightstand, my phone had the red light on it, blinking. I was in luck, it was from him. Both places that I inquired about were owned by W.C.W. Investments Ltd.

At my computer, I immediately typed in W.C.W. Investments Ltd. Moments later, I was looking at their home page. It featured a modern, two-story building. On the lawn, in front of it, was a sign that had the letters, W.C.W. on it. Under the letters, it read National Realtors and Investments. In smaller letters, it read, A Division of Landmark Developers.

I then looked up Landmark Developers. This time, the home page, featured a fancy logo, with the letters L.D. on it. Beneath that, was L.A. Enterprises. Once again, I gave it the ole college try! This time, there was a notice saying, that the site is temporarily closed.

OK, something fishy is going on, here! I've heard of businesses being under one huge umbrella, before, but this dive bar and a run-down motel, I don't think so! This thing must be bigger than I thought, and I'd bet my pension, that these bastards are funding the transportation and housing, for these girls. I immediately dialed the desk sergeant at the precinct.

"Sarge, it's me, Ricki."

"Detective, what can I do for you?"

"The Hispanic kid that was brought in earlier, with the tub of lard, for soliciting, are we still holding her?"

"Give me a minute and let me check."

I could hear him, striking the keys on his keypad.

"Nope, sorry, but she was released. It looks like, she made bail and has a hearing date."

"Damn! OK Sarge, I'll talk to you later."

CLICK.

I'll check later, but I'm sure that Cynthia Lewis posted bail for that kid. I'd love to talk to this kid, but I'm sure that she gave a false address, and then there's the language barrier. I'm thinking that wherever they're housing these girls, it can't be too far, from that motel.

15

MY PUNISHMENT

Mr. TJ, is next on my list of things to do. It's time to dissect this jerk and find out why, he isn't bench-pressing weights, in some prison yard. Someone is giving him a Get Out of Jail Free card, and I'm going to find out who they are. Before I could get started, I got a call from the captain.

"Ricki, I've got more good news, for you!"

"That's great, Captain!"

"Well, it may be a matter of opinion. Here's the deal. You're on a ninety-day probation period, and before you ask, I don't know which of the brass knuckleheads downtown, came up with this crap! You're going to be restricted to your desk, for a week. The Chief believes, that in a week, this whole mess will die down."

"Captain, I'm grateful for your efforts, and I know that I put myself in this position, but this is ridiculous! The humiliation that I'm going through, is more than enough, punishment. If I were one of the guys, I'd be getting a pat on the back! Anyway, Captain, I'll see you soon."

"It's a start, Ricki! Show them, by kicking ass!"

CLICK.

Now that I'm a free woman, so to speak, I locked up and headed for the station. I wanted to sit at the computer on my desk, and pull up

TJ's rap sheet, again. There must be some common denominator, or something, that I missed, before.

I didn't know what was going on, with the morning shift, but the squad room was empty. That was fine with me. It meant, that I could work in peace. Before I went into TJ's file, I decided to make copies of everyone's headshot, all for different reasons. The photos will include, my friend, Terri, Miss Kathy Johnson, the Hispanic kid, TJ, and Mr. Tommy G. Later on, each of them will come in handy.

Now, back to TJ. Reading his file the second time, was even more frustrating, than the first time. There was one thing that I was looking for, but could not find. The information regarding his involvement with the bar raid, years ago, was nowhere, to be found. Not a word, was mentioned. I made a note to myself, to talk to the Vice Squad, tomorrow.

On my third attempt at going through his file, something, caught my eye. The name, Cynthia Lewis, kept popping up, as his legal counsel. I made another note to myself, to check out the law firm of Lewis and Wilcox.

Since I was alone in the squad room, without anyone looking over my shoulder, I decided to bend the rules a little, and run a background check on Terri's parents. Neither of them had any history with law enforcement, which was a good thing. Employment-wise, her mom is a Bank Teller, and her dad is retired military, currently working as an Insurance Adjuster.

There was nothing that made the hairs on the back of my neck, stand, unless of course, he has a problem with discipline, from his military days. That kind of problem can make it difficult for Terri, to be daddy's little girl! There's a funny thing, about the city streets. They don't judge you, and they welcome you with the Devil's arms!

There was one more thing, that I wanted to do, before taking off. I went online to Lewis and Wilcox. As it turns out, their offices were out in south suburban Orland Park, out west, on Route 6. I wrote down the address and phone number. There's big-time clientele out there, where their offices are. Why in the hell, would they be getting their hands dirty, with trash, like TJ? I think that I'll pay them a little visit, and ruffle their feathers, some. Maybe, I can make this golden goose, lay a rotten egg!

I gathered up my things. I had one more stop to make, before leaving the station, and that was downstairs, to the tombs. It's time for round two, with Mr. Tommy G.

Near the entry door of the cell area, I put my sidearm in a lock box. I then showed my badge to the officer on duty, through the window. He buzzed me in and handed me a clipboard. I signed my name and printed the name of the scum bag, that I was visiting. Taking a quick look, up and down the clip board, indicated, that no lawyer, had come to see Tommy. I guess that means that when, and if, he makes bail, he'll be getting a Public Defender.

Tommy didn't look any worse than he had before, but he sure did smell worse, and it was plain to see, that being sober for so long, wasn't his cup of tea.

"So, Tommy, how's it going? I thought that your lawyer would've bailed you out by now! Come on, Tommy, make it easy on yourself."

"Why would I talk to you?"

"Because the sooner that you do, the sooner that you get to have that shot of whiskey, that you need."

He just sat on the steel bench, looking at me.

"So, tell me, how long have you and TJ been friends?"

"I don't know anyone, named TJ."

"Let me get this straight! You tend bar at Sally's. TJ and his biker pals drink at Sally's, but you don't know him. Is that right, Tommy?"

"I told you, I don't know anyone, named TJ."

"Well, let me show you something, Tommy."

I took out the picture of Terri from my file, and showed it to him.

"Now, Tommy, tell me that TJ didn't hook you up, with this kid, at that motel! Take a good look, before you answer. Either you or him, are going to jail for this crap!"

"I don't know anyone, named TJ!"

"That's fine with me Tommy, because I really don't care who does the stretch! Hey, you know what? I've got a better idea. Why don't I drop-in over at Sally's, and throw TJ's name around a bit, and tell people that you told me, that I could find him there?"

"You wouldn't do that!"

"OK, I guess that I'm wasting my time, here! I'll see you around, Tommy."

"You can't do this! They'll kill me!"

"Maybe I didn't make myself, clear. They don't serve whiskey in the joint, but they are very friendly with guys that do teenage kids!"

"OK, what do you want?"

"First of all, did TJ hook you up with the kid?"

"Can you guarantee me, that he won't find out that I, told you?"

"That depends on whether you're lying to me, because if you are, you can damn bet that he's going to find out! Now, one more time. Did he hook you up, with this kid?"

"Yeah, he did."

"Tell me what happened."

"Isn't that, enough?"

"Tommy, I can leave here when I get tired. You, on the other hand, when you get tired of it, you'll still be sitting here!"

"OK, I sat on the bed, waiting, while he fed the pipe to this chick. When he was done, he took off, and left us alone."

"What did you do to her, Tommy?"

"Nothing, I swear!"

That's when I got pissed and started yelling!

"Damnit, Tommy! I told you, not to lie to me!"

Before he could say anything, the officer on duty, came running to the cell.

"Is everything alright, here?"

"Yes officer, I just lost it for a moment, I'm sorry."

I waited for him to walk away, and go back to his desk.

"OK, Tommy, what did you do to her?"

"Alright, I tried, but she was so freaking stoned, that it was like being with a dead woman! She had no idea of where she was, or what she was doing. She was helpless! I got pissed, downed my whiskey, and threw the bottle on the sofa."

"What happened then, Tommy?"

"Like I said, I got pissed and took off, but I don't know jack, about a fire! That's the truth, I swear!"

"You know, Tommy. You're a real piece of crap! If I could, I'd shut you right now!

"Now, what happens?"

"You just wait, here."

I went back to the officer and borrowed an ink pen and pad. When I returned to the cell, Tommy was holding his face in his hands. Finally, he raised his head.

"You don't know, what you've done to me!"

"All I did is help you, help yourself, but for now, you're going to start from the top, and write it all down. Exactly the way that you told me."

I passed the pen and pad to him through the bars.

"Tommy, I'm going to step away again and leave you to finish that. I'll be back in a few minutes."

I stepped away, to spend a few minutes with the guard on duty.

That guy has been sweating bullets all-day, said the guard.

"What's he here for?"

"He was picked up at a motel, with an underage girl, but that's the least of his problems! He's tied to some really nasty people, and they hooked him up with this kid. He now believes that I'm going to feed him to the wolves."

"Well, if this guy is screwing around with kids, he deserves whatever he gets!"

"It's not, that I feel sorry for him, but he is cooperating with me. Even if the charges get reduced, he's still going to have to explain where he's been, because he works for these creeps!"

"Well, now I see why he's been sweating bullets. Oh well!"

I went back to Tommy's cell, and he gave me the pen and pad. I then stood, reading, what he'd written.

"OK, Tommy, this is what's going to happen. I'm going to give this to my captain, and we're going to do a little follow-up. For now, just sit tight, and I'm going to try and move this along, as fast, as I can."

I've never set anyone up to be gunned down on the street, and I have no intention of putting Tommy's name out there, but his life is what he made it. Honestly, I'd rather see him suffer, behind bars, just for being the kind of guy that he is.

I felt like, I had accomplished something, what exactly, I'm not sure of. What I do know, is, that TJ, is supplying the girls, and for some reason, I believe that Tommy G. doesn't know anything about the fire. The bottom line is, that he doesn't have the balls, to be hanging around with people like TJ. He's not a thug. He's just a horny old drunk!

16

THE STASH HOUSE

There was still some daylight, left. I wanted to see Terri as well as, take a ride past the address that was given by the Hispanic kid, known as Kathy Johnson. I figured that even if I ran out of daylight, I could still see Terri, so I decided to do the drive-by first.

I headed south, on Normal Ave., until I came up on 61st Street. I yielded, before making a left-hand turn. That's when a dark blue Crown Victoria came off 61st Street, turning north. Inside were two, not-so-undercover, dicks. They were cops that I didn't recognize, from my precinct. The way that they blew past me, I doubt that they noticed me. At the same time, I was thinking of how interesting it was that they'd be checking out the same street.

I dropped that thought, just as fast, as it entered my head. I had more important things, to think about. As I drove along the street, the first thing that caught my eye, was the number of beat-up, abandoned cars, that were there. It was obvious, that they'd been left behind, months ago, if not years. As I made my way further, down the street, I came across a two-story house, that had wide front steps, that led up to the porch, that matched the width of the house. Sitting on the top step, were three young girls. One of them was an African American kid, and the other two were Hispanic. As I slowly, passed by, the girls spotted me and quickly, ran inside the house. At that point, it was no reason for me, to hang around. My curiosity had been fed. I continued watching the house in my rear-view mirror.

While doing so, I got the shock of my life! There parked, just two doors down, from the house in question, was a Black, C Class Benz. The nerve of that son of a bitch! I wanted to slam on the breaks, rush in, and take TJ's ass, down! Without a warrant, it was just a fantasy, plus, I'm sure that when the girls ran inside the house, they set off some mental alarm. Even if I could find a judge, who would sign a warrant on my weak ass theory, I'm sure that the house would be vacant, by the time I got back. My hands are tied right now, but at least, Mr. TJ knows, that I'm on to his ass!

I figured that I may as well head over to the hospital, to see Terri. It was just about dusk when I arrived. When I walked into her room, she was sitting in a chair, looking out the window, with a portable IV stand, next to her. When she realized that I was present, she momentarily had an expression of gladness on her face, but she quickly let it go, and went back to her bad girl routine. I played it off and tried to make my visit seem casual.

"Do you mind, if I come in for a while?"

"Why not? I can't stop you!"

"Are you feeling better, today?"

"I guess, I don't know."

"What were you thinking about, before I, came in?"

"I wasn't thinking about, anything!"

"If I, were you, I'd be thinking about, when I can get the heck, out of here!"

"Well, you would be wrong! I have no place, to go!"

"Honey, you do have some place, to go."

 Our conversation wasn't going anywhere, so I shifted gears. I removed three of the photos from the file, that I'd put together. So far, during our little chit-chat, Terri had kept her back toward me, looking out the window. Before showing her the photos, I gave it one more shot.

"You could go back and hang out, with Kathy."

"I don't know, any Kathy!"

Standing behind her, I reached around and held the photo up, in front of her face. For a few moments, she stared at it, but then turned her head away.

"Are you sure, that you don't know her?"

"That's what I said, isn't it?"

"What if I told you, that she was arrested recently, for solicitation, and named you as her friend?"

"She couldn't have said that!"

"So, you do know her, and you also know that she can't speak, English!"

Terri stayed silent, looking out the window.

"Can I show you, another picture?"

Again, with the smart mouth!

"I can't stop you!"

I held the photo up.

"Do you know who, this guy is?"

It was a photo of Tommy G.

"No, I've never seen him before."

Considering the amount of meth that was in her system, when she was brought in, I believed her.

"He goes by the name of Tommy G. And guess what? He was busted, along with your friend, Kathy."

Terri didn't turn around and look at me, but she did, drop her head.

"You know what else, Terri? Tommy G. says that he was with you, at the motel, before it caught on fire."

That's when she lost it!

"Lies, lies, its all, just lies! I told you, that I don't know that guy!"

Watching her, sitting in that chair, crying, was the saddest thing in the world! No kid should be carrying this much on their shoulders, or have their poor precious bodies, deflowered by pigs, posing as men!

I planned to show her a picture of TJ, but it would've been too much for her. At this point, she had given me the pieces of the puzzle. It was now, up to me, to put it all together.

I stepped into her restroom and got a wet washcloth, so that she could wash her face. When I left her room, I had one thing on my mind. That was nailing Mr. TJ.

17

LATE-NIGHT CRUISING

On my way home, I went through a drive-through joint and picked up some sliders and a Coke. After eating, I went to my closet and pulled out a sleeveless jean jacket and a big box, filled with wigs. From my chest of drawers, I took out a red bandana.

Before changing, I called the captain to give him an update, on Tommy G.

"Hey Captain, it's me, Ricki."

"Good evening, Detective. I heard that you paid our boy a little visit, earlier."

"Yeah, I did."

"I hope that you have some good news, because we've got to either, charge this guy soon, or spring him."

"How about this, I've got a written confession."

"Good work, Detective!"

"However, there's a catch!"

"I should've known, it was! Let's have it."

"Captain, Tommy says that he was long gone when the fire started, and I believe him. He admits that the whiskey bottle was his. He even admits that he tried to have intercourse with Terri, but she was too wasted and out of it. According to him, he got pissed off, threw the bottle on the sofa, and took off."

"So, he just left her there, in that condition?"

"In his sick mind, there was nothing else that he could do. I've got to tell you, Captain. The doctor said that there was so much meth in her system, when she was brought in, that she had one foot in the grave! I hate to say it, but it's very possible that she unknowingly set that fire herself, trying to light the pipe."

"So, you're telling me, that the only thing, that we can nail this bastard for, is attempting to have sex with a minor?"

"Captain, there's no doubt in my mind, that this guy isn't a pig, but Attempted Murderer and Arson, I don't think so."

"OK, Ricki, I'll contact the D.A. and see if he thinks that he can sale it, and we'll release Tommy on his own, in the morning."

"Alright, Captain. In the meantime, I think that I'm on to something, and I'm following a hunch. I'll keep in touch with you.

CLICK.

It's been dark out, now, for a couple of hours and it's about time for me to go on my run. I took off my usual attire and slipped on a push-up bra with a black, low-cut, sleeveless shirt. Over my shirt, went my jean jacket. From my box of wigs, I chose a short-length brunette wig. After pinning up my hair, I pulled on the wig.

I was almost ready. All I needed was to wrap my bandana around the wig tightly, so that it doesn't come off. I took my badge out on my pocket and dropped it on my nightstand. I didn't want to be completely naked, so I took my backup pistol and clipped it to my boot leg holster. After pulling my pant leg down over it, I stood and looked at myself in the mirror.

The only thing, that I didn't like, was not wearing my helmet. Other than that, I looked just like the other scum, that hangs out at Sally's. Minutes later, I was downstairs, firing up my Sportster. It was a nice night for a ride, and the sensation from the wind, was great, even though I'm pro-helmet. There were quite a few people out on their bikes tonight, which I thought was cool.

After about twenty-five minutes into my ride, I could tell, that I was getting closer to Sally's. One way, that I could tell, was the number of Harleys, outnumbered the crotch rockets. Finally, I turned the corner, and about halfway down the block, three hogs were parked in front of Sally's. I could see through the windows that the place was packed, as I passed by. There had to be parking in the rear, so I continued and turned up an alley. The rear parking lot looked like, a freaking Harley convention!

I found the closest space that I could find, parked, and turned my bike off. I got off and looked at myself in the mirror, and out of the side of my eye, I saw a shiny new Jaguar. I thought to myself, that it sure looks out of place. It was parked at the far end, of all the bikes. I stood up, to get a better look, and saw more than I wanted to see! I couldn't believe my eyes! On the other side of the Jag, was the same dark blue Victoria, that I'd seen earlier. The hairs on the back of my neck, were standing up! I was actually having second thoughts, about going inside. Maybe they were casing the joint, just like I was, but for a different reason.

When I went inside, the place was full of smoke and loud music, which is the norm, for a joint, like this. Every stereotypical image, that I've ever heard of, was present in the place. There were even a couple of women that look like, they could bend steel, with their bare hands! I made a mental note, not to start any crap, with them.

I worked my way through the crowd, and pass a couple of pool tables, trying to get to one open stool, at the end of the bar. Along the way, I had to brush off a couple of unwanted, advances, but it was alright. They were just boys, being boys, after having a few beers. It took some effort, but I finally, made it. I waited about ten minutes, before a curly-haired, blonde bartender, showed up. She had tattoos, as far as the eye could see, a lit cigarette in her mouth, and the remains of a healing black eye.

"What will you have, honey?"

"I'll take a Jack, on the rocks."

Moments later, she brought my drink back. She then, took a long drag off her cigarette, and let the smoke out.

"I've never seen you here, before. You must be new, around these parts."

"Yeah, I guess that you can say that."

I put a ten spot on the bar and told her to keep it.

"So, what brings you in?"

"Some guy, that I ran into some time back, told me about the place."

"Oh yeah, what's his name?"

"Honey, you can never tell with these guys, but he goes by Tommy G. To be honest, with you, he was a real scum bag!"

"I've been working here, for years, and I can't recall any, Tommy G."

"Yeah well, you're not missing much!"

She excused herself, walked down to the center of the bar, and picked up the telephone receiver. Her conversation lasted less than a minute. Behind the bottles of liquor on the wall, was a mirror. In the view behind me, were stairs leading up to what I thought, was an office.

After realizing that the stairs were there, I couldn't help but look at them, every two or three minutes. I knew that Blondie had lied to me, so I downed by shot, and was about to leave, when the door to the office opened. The first guy that stepped out, was a tall Hispanic man, wearing a well-tailored, tan-colored, western-styled suit, complete with a matching Stetson cowboy hat. Even his rattlesnake, brown boots, were the real thing! They had to cost upward of 900.00 dollars. And I thought that I was out of place!

Had I been downing my Jack, right now, I would've choked on it, because coming down behind this guy, with beers in their hands, were the two dicks that belonged to the dark blue Vicki, outside. I didn't know what I had stumbled into, but I thought that I'd better get the hell out of there! When the last of the trio got to the bottom step, he stopped for a moment, and stared at my reflection in the mirror. Damn it!

I pretended not to notice him, as they headed out the rear door. I gave it a few minutes, and then headed out the rear door, myself. All the time, I was wondering, if this cop had recognized me, even with this wig on. It could be, that Blondie, tipped him off, about me mentioning Tommy. That would explain, her quick phone conversation.

I made a beeline for my bike, and as I was pulling out, I could see the three men sitting in the Jag with the light on. As I turned out of the alley, I didn't know if I'd made a narrow escape, or they were letting me leave on purpose.

About six blocks, away from Sally's, I got my answer. In my mirror, I could see three hogs, coming up behind me, fast. I didn't think that trying to outrun them, was a good option. When they caught up with me, one of them, came around and got in front of me, purposely, slowing down. The other two, came up on my right side.

The one right beside me, started to creep over closer to me. In one motion, he raised his left foot, and took a quick look behind himself. That's when I nailed his ass, before he could get me! Using my right foot, I gave his bike a hard shove.

He went straight, into a death wobble, and lost control. He then, ended up flipping over, into his buddy's bike. Both guys, and their bikes, went ass-over-elbow, across the pavement! The lead jerk in front of me, heard the commotion and turned his head around to see what, was going on. That's when he crossed the double yellow lines,

and went head-on, into the grill of a car, that had already stopped, trying to avoid him. He came off his bike, and sailed, right through the car's windshield. That left me an opening! I counted my blessings and hauled ass, home!

18

LEWIS AND WILCOX

When I got back to my place, the first thing that I did, was pour myself a strong one! I needed to calm my nerves. Too much, was happening, and I didn't know why. Those three creeps that tried to take me out, were a major overkill. All, because I mentioned a small fish, like Tommy G. Obviously, I'd poked a hornet's nest. In general, when someone attempts to kill in the public, they've got something to hide. No doubt, they were sending me a message. They didn't like me sticking my nose into their business, and the easiest way for them to stop me, was to kill me. Surely, their investment is far more valuable, than my life.

I got out of my crazy get-up and took a seat in my recliner. I then grabbed the remote and turned on the TV. I wasn't too surprised, to see that the incident was already getting live news coverage, by the local media. I caught the tail end of the reporter's spin.

WITNESSES SAY THAT THERE WAS A FOURTH BIKER INVOLVED. POSSIBLY A WOMAN THAT FLED THE SCENE.

In the background, I could see a fire engine, two ambulances, and at least, three squad cars. On the ground, was a body, covered with a tarp. The other two guys were on gurneys and being treated at the scene. The whole area was taped off, and there were flares lying on the ground, blocking off the street, in both directions.

I've never been happy, to hear about someone, losing their life, especially when I'm involved, but someone, gave these creeps the order, to take my life. I'm an officer of the law, foremost, and even if I weren't, I don't think that the world, is going to feel a damn bit, sorry, for these bastards!

I turned off the TV, and just sat there. The next thing that I knew, it was nearly, 3:00am. That's when I got up and went to bed. When I woke the next morning, it seemed like, a typical day. I was beginning my normal routine, and then suddenly, the events of last night, hit me.

Another thing, that crossed my mind, was the fact that I may not be out of the woods yet. The way that I see it, is, if these people already wanted me dead, how do they feel, knowing that I took out, three of their own? I want to go to the captain, but he's not going to like, what I did. When I clock in, to the mid-shift this afternoon, it'll be the first of restricted days, at my desk. I have until 3:00 PM before my shift starts, and it's nearly 9:00 AM now. I think that I'll take a run, out to Orland Park, and see what I can get, out of Lewis and Wilcox. If things go well, maybe I'll even have time, to check in on Terri, again.

Most cops would think that I'm out of my mind, for working an investigation on my own time. The way that I see this case is, there's people out there making money off the abuse of these young girl's bodies, and they don't take time off! The time that I would be sitting on my ass, waiting for my shift to start, is more than enough time, for some young girl, to lose her life to a filthy, scum bag.

I do understand officers that want to be compensated, for a hard day's work. To me, saving a life, is far more valuable, than a fat check.

I got dressed and hit the streets, heading for the I-57 Expressway. Fortunately, for me, I was going southbound. The northbound side of the expressway was packed with traffic, headed downtown. The cherry on top, the highway would be clear, on my way back. After a twenty-five-minute ride, I got off the expressway at 159th Street, and went west, toward Orland Park. The luscious green trees of the suburbs, made me feel like, I was in another world. It was hard to believe, that a booming metropolis, like the city of Chicago, was just minutes away. It wasn't long, before small businesses started popping up, and that led to apartment complexes and strip malls.

I pulled into a gas station and parked my bike. After grabbing a cup of coffee, I went back to my bike, leaned against it, and went through my notes, in search of the address of the law firm. Ten minutes later, my coffee was gone, and I was back in the flow of traffic. The firm is on the main drag, in the six hundred-block of Route 6. Sitting at a traffic signal, I could see a five-story commercial building, a little over two blocks, down the street. As I approached the building, I saw near the parking lot entrance, a large granite sign. It was engraved with the words, Orland Park Professional Plaza. On the left side of the building, was a well-manicured lawn, with Old Glory, flying on a pole.

I pulled into the lot and parked my bike. I took off my helmet, and let my hair loose, before locking it to my bike. As I walked through the parking area, toward the main entrance, I thought that my eyes were playing tricks on me. As I passed a roll of parked vehicles, just four spaces from the end, was a shiny new Jaguar, identical to the one that was parked at Sally's, last night. I was thinking no, it can't be! This time, I had an opportunity, which I didn't have last night. I walked over, to write down the plate number, but before I could, I spotted a beautiful, tan-colored Stetson cowboy hat, on the front seat.

Well, I'll be damned!

Now, there's no doubt in my mind, that this firm and Sally's are sleeping together. I didn't know who could've been watching me, from an office window, so I quickly wrote down the plate number, and made my way toward the entrance.

The moment, that I stepped into the lobby, it was quite apparent, that someone, had paid a decorator, a king's ransom, to lay this place out! All the furnishings were lavish designer imports. Even the walls were covered with a fabric wallpaper, that I've never seen before. In a glass enclosure, mounted on the wall, beside the elevator, was a marquee. It displayed the services in the building, and the floors that they were on.

There were Optometrists, Dentists, Tax Accountants, Chiropractors, and even an Architectural Firm. This building housed the who's who, of big money services. The firm of Lewis and Wilcox was listed on the fourth floor. I pressed the elevator button and waited. Moments later, a soft, female voice, said, Main Lobby.

Wow, these guys spared no expense!

When I stepped off the elevator, the firm, was right across the hall. The office exterior wall was made of glass, with the door, in the center. To the left of the door, painted in gold metal flake, Old English letters, was the name, Lewis and Wilcox, Attorneys at Law. I stepped through the door and was greeted by a male receptionist, who appeared to be gay.

His mannerism was very professional. Not a hair on his head was out of place, and his nails were perfectly manicured. His clothes were designer, and his attitude was impeccable. Hell, I would've hired him too!

He wore an ultra-thin modern headset, that had a flexible thin tube that followed the contour of his face, with a mouthpiece on the end. Just as I was about to speak, he must've gotten an incoming call, because he motioned for me, to hold on a minute. He finished his phone conversation, and stood up from his desk, extending his hand to me.

"I'm sorry, about that! Good morning, and welcome to Lewis and Wilcox, Attorneys at Law."

"Good morning to you, too."

"How may I assist you, Miss…

"Oh, I'm sorry. I'm Detective Ricki Cliff, with the Chicago Police Department."

I took out my badge and showed it to him.

"How may I assist you, Detective Cliff?"

"I'd like to speak with, Cynthia Lewis."

"Do you have an appointment, with her, this morning?"

"No, I don't, but I won't take up much, of her time."

"Do you mind, taking a seat, Detective? I'll tell her, that you're here."

"Thank you."

As he spoke into his mouthpiece, I took a seat on a black, leather lounge, and picked up a copy of News Week magazine, from the nearby end table. Before I could open it, he spoke to me, again.

"Excuse me, Detective, she's finishing up a meeting, and she'll be out in a moment."

"Thank you."

"May I offer you, some coffee, or tea?"

"No thank you, I'm fine."

I went back to the magazine and started thumbing through the pages. Just as I was getting into an article on the sky rocketing cost of a college education, I was interrupted.

"Good morning, Detective Cliff. I'm sorry, for keeping you waiting."

Standing before me, was a brunette, with her hair in a bun. She was about 5'-10", maybe 5'-11" with the slender body of a model. Her skin, looked as smooth, as a baby's butt, and behind her designer glasses, were an incredible pair of gray eyes. If it wasn't for the traditional pin-striped business suit, I would've thought, that she was a model, posing as a lawyer, instead of, the other way around.

"Hi, it's a pleasure to meet you, Miss Lewis."

"Please, join me in our conference room."

Once in the conference room, I was again offered coffee or tea, but this time, bottled water was added to the menu.

"So, what brings the Chicago Police Department, all the way out here, to our little town?"

"Well, I was doing some research on a gentleman, that's related to a case, that I'm working on."

"If you don't mind me, asking, what is the nature, of this case?"

"It involves a teenage girl, that was left unconscious, in a burning building."

"I must say, Detective, that's horrible, but I'm curious, how did your investigation, lead to me?"

"While doing background research, on one of the suspects, I noticed, that you've represented him, on more than one occasion."

"Oh really, can you tell me the name, of this guy?"

"His name is Thaddeus James, A.K.A. TJ."

At this point, she pretended not to know, who, I was talking about.

"I'm sorry, but the name doesn't ring a bell. Can you give me a moment, please?"

She went to a phone, on a nearby desk, picked it up, and asked that TJ's file, be brought in.

"Detective, do you mind if I ask, what exactly, your interest in my client, is?"

Suddenly, she knew who I was talking about. Go figure!

Before I could answer, her receptionist walked in and gave her the file. I knew that when she sat down and started looking at it, she was just going through the motions, on my behalf.

"I've noticed that over the years, you not only, represented Mr. James, but you've got him off, on some very questionable crimes."

"Detective, I'm sure that you know, that due to confidentiality, I can't go into details. I can tell you, that according to our records, it appears that the D. A., had rather poor, evidence, against Mr. James."

"Counselor, don't you find it the least bit strange, that he's walked away, repeatedly?"

"Honestly, Detective, we do our best for our clients, but we still have to follow the guidelines of the system. If he's a free man, it's because of the system, itself."

"As long as we're being honest, Counselor, you should know, that I have evidence, that your client, is involved in three felonies, and more than likely, we'll be seeing each other, again!"

"Detective, if that's all, I really have a full schedule, today."

That was her polite way of saying, get out!

"I do have one more, question. How does a small-time thug, like James, bankroll a firm, like yours?"

"As I said earlier, Detective, that's confidential."

"Well, thank you for your time, Miss Lewis. I'll be going, now."

I didn't know, if Miss Lewis thought that I was just a rookie, that was still green, or what, but that little trick that she pulled with the telephone was the oldest scam, in the book! I knew that she activated the intercom, and my Hispanic Cowboy, was in another room, listening to our conversation. She escorted me back to the lobby, and I took off.

19

SURPRISE!

While I was out, making nice, with the good folks at Lewis and Wilcox, Mr. Tommy G. was being released, on his own, from the lock-up. He took off, walking, in search of the nearest bus stop. He could finally, relax and get that shot of whiskey, he's been dying, to have. When he stepped off the bus, in his neighborhood, a black Benz, went past him, and pulled over to the curb. It stopped, about three car lengths ahead of him. He saw the car and said, damn it! He knew that it was TJ, and he also knew, that he had seen him. He couldn't turn back, and he couldn't run away. When he reached the Benz, the passenger window went down.

"Tommy G., my man! Hop in, partner! Let me treat you to lunch?"

"I really need to get home, TJ. Maybe, another time."

TJ wasn't buying it, and insisted that Tommy get into the car. With no other option, he nervously, worked his over-sized body, into the Benz.

"So, what's been happening, Tommy? We miss you, over at Sally's, man!"

"Yeah, I've been lying low, not feeling too, good."

"You know, a lot has been happening the last few days. Two of our brothers were killed on their bikes, last night. One's going to be in the hospital for freaking ever! To make matters worse, some female cop has been snooping around. You wouldn't know anything, about that, would you, Tommy?"

"That's all news, to me, TJ."

Tommy knew that TJ knew, that he was lying to him, and he was just about to pee in his pants. There was no way that their little meeting, could have a happy ending.

"What about my girl, Kathy? I know that you know about that."

"Yeah, the cops busted her, after we hooked up."

"Oh yeah, and they just let you, walk away?"

"That's the way that it went down, TJ, I swear!"

"Well, that's cool Tommy, but I've got a question. What happened in that motel, after I left you with Terri?"

"Nothing, freaking happened! She was too wasted, to do anything, so, I just left her, there."

Inside, TJ was steaming, because Tommy, had put the heat on him, and his superiors had given him the order, to fix his problem! Tommy looked at TJ and asked where they were going, for lunch.

"I figured that we could drop by the park, take a seat, and finish talking, first."

"Finish talking, about what, TJ?"

"Relax, it's all good, my man!"

TJ pulled into the park's parking area and got out of the car. Tommy, just sat there, until TJ walked around and opened his door.

"Come on, Tommy, there's a picnic bench, right over there."

He got out and started walking, slowly. TJ pointed, and Tommy walked in that direction, with TJ behind him. As they headed for the bench, TJ began talking and looking around, at the same time.

"You know, Tommy, two of my road dogs are dead, plus, I've lost one of my working girls. That's a lot of damn money, Tommy!"

Tommy wanted to plead his case, but before he could say anything, he felt a sharp blade stick into his kidneys. As he tried pulling away, TJ yanked the knife, slicing all the way around, to his stomach.

94

You no good, fat ass, piece of shit, screamed TJ!

While Tommy lay on the ground, bleeding out, TJ kicked him in the side, not realizing, that he'd broken a rib, sending it straight, into one of Tommy's lungs. He took another look, around, and headed back to his car, leaving Tommy G., lying on the ground. He looked just like, another homeless guy, napping in the park.

In the meantime, I had several things on my mind, during my drive back to Chicago. I couldn't wait, to run a DMV check on the Jaguar, and find out who the Hispanic cowboy is. So far, on the surface, there are some major players, in this game, and soon, rather I want to, or not, I'm going to have to go to the captain. I'm used to working alone, but if thing, is as big, and widespread, as I think that it is, working alone, will be the equivalent, of taking a knife to a gunfight!

Another thing, on my mind, is Terri and her parents. I've got contacts, with Social Services, and even though her parents may be willing, when she's released, I know that I've got as much chance, of talking her into family counseling, as a snowball in hell has! If only, this kid could see that her parents, are her best friends. Maybe, if I take at a shot at Terri's mom, we can work as a team and get to this kid. One thing for sure, I'm definitely, putting the miles on my bike today. After leaving Orland Park, I'm now in-route to a small Savings and Loan, located in one of the suites in the old, Ford Shopping Mall. It's been a long time, since I've passed through the town of Cicero. I can remember riding through this area with my dad, and seeing a Tootsie Roll candy factory, while in route to Midway Airport. As a kid, seeing that factory, was the highlight of the trip. It's sad, that my trip today, is to pull on the heart strings, of Mrs. Wallace, regarding the future of her daughter.

I'm not a mom, but I can imagine how it's going to feel, when I add pain to that, which she has already endured. I see it as a necessary, evil. Unfortunately, Mrs. Wallace will have to go through more pain, to get pass this episode in her daughter's life.

I pulled off of Cicero Ave. and into the mall's parking lot. All, that I had to do now, was find the entrance to the Savings and Loan. After cruising around, a little, I found it. There was no need in me going inside, have her co-employees see that she has business with the police, not to mention, that she may get emotional. It's near noon, and I'm hoping that maybe, she'd step out, for lunch. I parked and waited. While waiting, my cellphone vibrated. It was the captain, once again, calling me, while I'm off duty.

"Good morning, Cap, what's up?"

"Good morning, Detective. Have you been doing any freelance work, on your own time?"

Now, why in the hell, would he be asking me that, out of the blue?

"I've done a little bit, but not, much."

Of course, I was lying.

"Why are you, asking?"

"We've got a problem, and it's a Vice problem!"

"That sounds serious, Captain."

"It is, and you're not going to like it! You can come in now, or you can wait, until you clock in."

"Please, don't tell me, that this is about, Councilman Lee!"

"No, Ricki, but I wish that it were."

"Damn it, Captain, why can't I catch a break? I'm going to drop what I'm doing, and shut right over, there."

CLICK.

I had to take a powder on my little get-together, with Mrs. Wallace. The captain, really had my mind, spinning. What the hell, could I have done, now? There is no way in hell, that Vice could know that I had something to do, with those bikers. A verity of possibilities, went through my mind, while I was driving, but none, that made sense. My only knowledge of Vice, is that raid, that took place, years ago, and I wasn't involved in that. Seeing that the captain wasn't yelling and screaming, at me, I kinda get the feeling, that I haven't done anything wrong. I guess I'll find out, soon.

20

STAND DOWN, DETECTIVE

By the time I made it to the station, it was near 1:30 PM. As I was pulling into the parking lot, on one end, there were three squad cars, screaming out the other. That in itself, wasn't unusual, but it did catch my eye. When I walked into the lobby, I was greeted by the desk sergeant, but his mood was a little dry. I looked around, to see if anyone was paying attention to us, and then walked up, to his counter.

"What's going on, Sarge?"

"I'm not sure, but the Cap, got a visit from the A.D.A., this morning, and he hasn't been the same, since."

"OK, thanks."

First, it was the Vice Squad, and now it's the Assistant District Attorney. What the hell, is going on? Now, that I think of it, why would the captain, tell me, that I'm not going to like it? What I like, or don't like, has never mattered, before! I was completely baffled, as I headed upstairs. When I walked into the squad room, the Captain was standing in the doorway of his office, as if, he were waiting for me.

"Come on in, Detective, and close the door, behind yourself."

Man, no hellos, no put your things down, first, no nothing! If I didn't know better, I'd think that I was about to be, terminated. I did, as I was told. I closed his office door, and took a seat.

"What's going on, Captain?"

"Detective, there's no easy way to tell you this, so I'm just going, to say it. I'm ordering you, to back off of TJ."

I immediately, jumped out of my seat!

"What the hell, Captain! This is bullshit! Why do I have to back off of that, asshole?"

"That did not come from me, Ricki! It came from, downtown."

"But, why Captain, he's the keystone, to this mess! Why the hell, are they doing this, to us?"

"I had a meeting with the A.D.A., this morning, and it was after, he had met with the Chief."

"So, what the hell, does that have to do, with Vice?"

"Apparently, years ago, when that biker bar, Sally's, was raided by Vice, a deal was cut."

"Jesus Captain, please don't say, what I'm thinking!"

"Mr. TJ turned state's evidence that helped the Feds nab a very, big fish. Basically, Vice and the Feds were working together, but the Feds stayed in the shadows. Now Detective, I need you to listen, very closely. I know that you've been doing some freelance, regarding the case."

"But Captain!"

"Let me finish! Recently, you've spoken to the wrong person, and you threw Mr. TJ's name around, with a little pressure. Whoever, that person was, they pulled some strings, with Vice. To make a long story, short, they used the A.D.A., as a messenger boy. Now, you can speak."

"Captain, if I start from the beginning, you don't have time to let me speak! First, you'll need a recorder. Second, this thing is far bigger than I dreamed, and you'll definitely want another agency, in on this!"

The captain, then lowered his face, into his hands. After a few moments, he raised his head, back up.

"My God, Ricki, what have you got us into, this time?"

"What, would you say, to Pimping, Prostitution, Human Trafficking, and Racketeering?"

"You're right, Ricki. I don't have the time or the resources!"

"Captain, I can damn near, prove, that what I'm saying, is true. You can get whoever, you want, to sit in, and I'll start from the beginning. In the meantime, I want to make a move."

The captain was just about to lose it, when his phone, rang.

Now, what is it, he yelled!

"This is Captain Keller, speaking."

SILENCE.

"Yeah, yeah, Jesus Christ! When it rains, it pours! OK, tape off the area, and go through the normal routine. I'm on my way!"

CLICK.

"What is it, Captain?"

"Ricki, we'll finish this, whatever it is, later. Come on, you're coming with me!"

"What's going on?"

"It's Tommy G."

I had a feeling that something awful happened to Tommy. This time, I lowered my face into my hands. I felt like I put a contract hit, out on this man.

"Oh my God, Captain, it's my fault!"

"No, it's not your fault! More than likely, someone else, put the word out, that he was released. Now, shake it off! That's an order! He was found in the park. Witnesses say, that they thought that he was a sleeping, homeless man. Come on, let's see what we can get from the M.E."

The Captain and I went downstairs to the Motor Pool, and took off in an unmarked squad. The Captain was rather quiet, while we were driving, and it was making crazy! I had to say, something.

"What do you want me, to do, Captain?"

"For starters, you can give me some of the major details, things that stand out."

"There is so much, that I don't know where to start. I'm just going to ramble, and you can stop me, when you want. The motel, that caught on fire, is owned by the same company that owns Sally's bar. That company is under the umbrella of another company, that is yet again, under the umbrella of another company, in Mexico. That's where the trail ends. I have reason to believe that TJ's working girls are the result of human trafficking, from south of the border. These companies, are funding the transportation of the girls. You know Captain, I can stop here, if you'd like."

"Detective, I only have one problem. I thought that we were Narcotics!"

"I know what you're thinking, Captain, but this mess started with my investigation into the near overdose, of Terri Wallace. Once that the trail led to TJ, all kinds of crazy things, started happening!"

"Like what, Detective?"

"Like TJ's rap sheet, that goes way back. He's beaten every one of his cases, and in each case, he was represented by Lewis and Wilcox at Law. This is a big-time, Gucci, firm, that's way out, in Orland Park. How is it, that a small-time pimp, can afford, these people?"

"We need more than that, Detective."

"You want more, I'll give you, more! The kid, that was busted at the motel, with Tommy, I went to the address that she gave us, and guess what? There, sitting on the porch, were more teenage girls! They took one look at me and hauled ass! As I drove by, there was TJ's shiny Black, C Class Benz, parked right out in front, of the freaking place!"

"What else, do you have, Detective?"

"When I first pulled up, to the street, I passed two plain cloths dicks, in a Vicki."

"That doesn't mean, anything!"

"Oh no, I went to Sally's bar, the other night."

"What the hell, were you doing there?"

"Captain, while I was sitting there, a door to an office opened, and this tall, well-dressed Hispanic guy, stepped out, and who do you think, steps out, behind him? It was the two dicks, that were in the Vicki!"

"Are you sure, Detective?"

"Yes, I'm sure, and I'd bet my life, that the two dicks, are Vice! The big Hispanic guy, wears a tan-colored Stetson cowboy hat, and drives a new Jaguar. If you like what you've heard so far, I can keep going, because it gets better!"

"Jesus, Detective, you scare the hell out of me sometimes! I know that I'm going to regret this, but go ahead!"

"OK, so one of these two dicks, thinks that he recognizes me, and I play him off. The next thing, that I know, I've got three guys on Harleys, surrounding me, trying to spread my brains, across the freaking pavement!"

"Wait, a minute! Does this have anything to do, with those guys that were killed the other night?"

"Hell yes, it does! I took those assholes out, before they could kill me!"

"For the love of God, Ricki, you've got to stop doing crap, like this! You can't just kill people, and drive off, into the freaking sunset!"

"How the hell, did I know, that they were going to die? Maybe, if they weren't trying to kill me, they'd still be alive!"

"Do you realize, that the department has officers out there, investigating that incident? And now, that you've told me, that makes me an accessory!"

"Well, I'm sorry Captain, but do you have any concern at all, that these people may have something to hide, and they were trying to kill me, so that they can keep it, hidden?"

"Of course, I'm concerned, but this is a mess! What am I, supposed to do, pull our guys off the investigation, and tell them, that one of our cops was involved and fled the scene, or better yet, just let them continue to waste the tax payers' money?"

"It's not that I don't care, Captain, but we both know, that there's a damn good chance, that these three bastards, had rap sheets, and in the end, it's going to go in the books, as just another hit and run."

"That may be so, but in the mean-time, I've got to think about, this crap! Is there anything else, Detective?"

"Yeah, there's one more major detail. This morning, I paid a visit to Lewis and Wilcox."

"Bingo! That's who pulled the strings!"

"Oh, so now, you believe me!"

"I never said, that I didn't believe you, but why in the hell, were you screwing around, with those people?"

"I wanted to know, how they were able, to keep bouncing a punk, like TJ."

"Yeah, well, I'm sure that they told you, that it was confidential."

"Yeah, you're right, but my big Hispanic friend, from Sally's, had his Jag parked in their lot, and I know that it was him, because I saw his Stetson, sitting on the front seat. My next move was going to be running a D.M.V. check, to find out who this guy is."

"That's good work, Detective! From now on, rather you're on, or off duty, anytime, that you're in the public, I want you wearing your vest. That's an order, and please, this time, will you follow my damn orders?"

"Well, Captain, that's the fat details."

"Yeah, well, that's enough for now. The problem is, that I don't know who the hell to trust! Don't say another word about this, to anyone. I've got to think, for a while."

Once again, it was quiet, and I swear, I could hear the wheels turning, in the captain's head. It never dawned on me, that I was fleeing the scene of an accident. At the time, all that I could think about, was saving my own ass!

Two blocks, down the street, I could see blue lights, flashing on top of the same three squads, that I saw leaving the station, earlier. As we got closer, there were small groups of people, staring into the park. I imagine, that they'd been pushed back, to the perimeter. We slowly pulled in and parked, behind one of the squads. The captain grabbed his hand-held radio, and we got out.

We walked through the groups of onlookers, and before we got within 30 yards, of the police tape, we could see the large outline, of Tommy G., under a plastic tarp. When we reached the edge of the tape, I paused, for a moment.

"You know, Detective. You don't have to do this, if you don't want to."

"That's OK, Cap, I'm ready."

He lifted the tape, and we both bent down and stepped under it. One of the uniformed officers greeted us, right away.

"We've got a bad one, Cap. The victim is Mr. Thomas Garner, a 36-year-old, African American male. There was no money on him, but he did have this."

The officer gave the captain a small folded, piece of yellow paper. He opened it and saw, that it was Tommy's bail ticket receipt.

Captain, this guy has either got some serious bad luck, or whoever did this, knew that we were releasing him this morning, said the officer. The captain and I gave each other a strange look.

"Thank you, officer, you can return to what you were doing."

Hey Cap, I said.

"I'd bet a dollar to a donut, that the Vice guys gave TJ, the 411!"

"As much as I hate to, I'm inclined to agree with you."

We walked over to the body, to see what the M.E., had to say.

"Well, well, Captain Keller, so we meet, again!"

This is Detective Cliff, said the captain.

"Do you mean, the famous, Detective Cliff?"

"Cut the crap! What do we have?"

"We have a 35 to 38-year-old Black male. He was sliced from the kidneys, almost, all the way around to his navel. He bled out, in a matter of minutes. I'd say, that he's been dead, for at least, seven hours. I'll be able to tell you more, later on."

"Thanks, Doc. OK Detective, there's nothing else, that we can do here. We may as well, head back, and do me a favor, Ricki."

"What's that, Cap?"

"Just sit at your desk, and work! Don't get pissed, and shut the vending machine, or throw hot coffee, on one of those jerks, that you work with!"

"Sure, Cap."

21

KEEPING IT IN THE FAMILY ⏤⏤⏤

I sat at my desk and tried to behave, as the captain requested. I wanted to focus on this case, instead of the officers sitting around the squad room, with me. My computer was fired up and waiting for me, to ask it something, so I ran a D.M.V. report on the cowboy's Jaguar. As it turns out, the vehicle is registered to Mr. Rafael Esteban Petreas, of Country Club Hills.

I also found, that the vehicle is leased, from Orland Park Luxury and Performance Vehicles. It's a high-end dealership that carries makes like, BMW, Mercedes, Range Rovers… I made a note to myself, to find out, who's footing the monthly leasing fee. One thing for sure, the law firm and the dealership, are just a little, too close, for my comfort zone.

I figured that as long as I had access, to the DMV's database, I'd back track, and take another look at Mr. TJ's Benz. I have a funny feeling. A few key strokes, and bang! My instincts were right, and it appears that his Benz is also leased from the Orland Park dealership. The cherry on top was, that it's also registered at the Country Club Hills address.

This is too good, to be true! Why would this firm, be bending over backward, for these guys? At the moment, I don't know what it would take, to find out, who's footing the lease on these cars, but I do have a way of finding out, the name of the person, living in the Country Club Hills residence. If there's a house, apartment, or condo, at the address given, then they're going to need electricity. One call, to Common Wealth Edison, will verify the resident's name. I wasted no time, in doing so. I contacted Edison, and after being transferred twice, I finally, got a Customer Service Supervisor, on the line. After verifying that I was with the department, the supervisor entered the address, into her computer.

"Thank you for waiting, Detective Cliff. Our records indicate, that the service provided at the address you've given me, is billed to a Mr. David Wilcox."

For a moment, I was dumbfounded.

"Detective, are you still there?"

"Yes, yes, I'm here! Thank you for your time."

CLICK.

This damn thing is starting to get fishier, than Lake Michigan! I'd been wondering, what part, Wilcox played, in this game. I have two expensive vehicles, leased from the same dealer, and registered to an address where neither of the drivers, live at. I've heard of lawyers, going out of their way, to protect the privacy of their clients, but this is, way over the top! There has to be more to this Wilcox guy, than meets the eye. I'm going to start out, the easy way, by running a background check on him, and see what pops up. After that, I'm going to run a little scam, on Mr. Efficient, the receptionist, out at Lewis and Wilcox.

When I entered Mr. Wilcox into the department's database, which is linked to the state's data base, there were at least a dozen or more people, with the same name. That's when I got comfortable in my seat, and started working from the top, down. What I found, was a David Wilcox, of all ages. Some were deceased, and some were locked up already. Finally, I saw a David that was attached to Lewis and Wilcox. It turns out, that Mr. Wilcox passed the Bar Exam in 1991, and earned his degree at DePaul University, where he majored in Criminal Justice, with a minor in Immigration Law. The subject of Immigration Law was ringing a bell, in my head, but I didn't know, why.

Moving along, there were no records, of any criminal offenses, with law enforcement. To me, that only meant, that he's never been caught. There was no marital history, or mention of siblings. As a kid, he graduated from Thornridge High School, in Dolton, Illinois. It also appears that that's where he spent, his childhood. The trail ended there, which was strange. Going backward, I got as far as, three years old. There was no other record of him, before the age of three. Also, there was no place of birth, and no parents listed. My past experience tells me, that more than likely, he was a foster kid, and his records are sealed. If I'm going to get any further, with this, I've got to go around the I.N.S., and go straight to Immigration and Customs Enforcement. Even, then, I'm going to need special help. Along with the right person, pulling some strings, I'm going to need a damn good reason, for that person, to risk their neck, for me!

I swear, sometimes it seems like the trust between the criminals on the street, is far better, than that of the different government departments! There's nothing, that I can do, at this point. Next up, is my little game, with the receptionist, at the law firm. Before dialing, I mentally prepared myself, for using my college intern, bubbly voice. I took a deep breath, as I listened to the phone ringing, on the other end.

"Good afternoon, thank you for calling Lewis and Wilcox, Attorneys at Law. How may I assist you, today?"

"Hi, I'm Cindy, calling from Orland Park Luxury and Performance Vehicles! I'm with the award-winning customer service team. If you don't mind, sir, I have a few questions, regarding the recent service that you've received. It'll only take a minute of your time."

"Can you hold, please?"

He didn't really, put me on hold. It was more like, he partially covered the microphone, with his hand, because I could hear a man's voice, telling him to say that everything is great. I assumed, that that voice belonged to Mr. Wilcox.

"I'm back. Thank you for holding. Now, how may I help you?"

"Well sir, our records show that among other vehicles, you've recently leased a Mercedes C Class and a Jaguar. All that I need to know is, are you happy with the performance of the vehicles and the service that our associates, have been providing?"

"Everything is going great, and we're very satisfied."

"Thank you so much, for your time, sir, and remember, that if you need anything, please give us a call. Bye!"

CLICK.

Wow, that was too easy! No wonder millions of dollars are made every day, on telephone scams! I swear, if I ever get into trouble, I'm going to call these guys! Hell, every client gets a new car! It's not that I doubted the DMV records, but I just wanted to hear it from the horse's mouth.

22

HUMAN TRAFFICKING 101

Before my shift ends, I need to begin creating a time and date log of everything I've discovered, regarding this case, from day one. Whoever, the captain decides to bring in, is going to need to know the details. It'll be a lot easier, than me, telling that person everything, from the beginning. Logging everything in numerical order is going to take time, and there's no way, that I can sit here and do it all, at once. What I really want to do, is take a couple of hours to go online and educate myself on the Mexican Cartel, and human trafficking. They're both, ugly subjects, and honestly, I'm afraid of what I'm going to learn.

I started by simply, typing in the words, human trafficking. There were dozens of sites, devoted to this subject. As I scrolled down the pages, one in particular, caught my eye, because the research supporting the information given, was done at DePaul University, College of Law. I fell back in my chair as chills began running through my body. The first thought that came to my mind was Mr. Wilcox. I know that it's a shot, in the dark, but could he possibly, be this cold and devious? I really have no proof that he's tied to TJ's girls, but I can imagine the success these guys would have, knowing a lawyer that could guide them around the long arm of the law.

I doubt that he was the analyst at the university, that did the actual research, but the fact that he minored in Immigration Law, and obviously has something going on with these creeps, is a bit, too much. I continued reading, and found that the case studies in this research, were based on interviews with actual participants, in the sex trade. It was shocking to find, that a great deal of these women were homegrown, and fell victim to someone that they knew and trusted. I was getting educated alright, but I needed to learn more about the cartel's involvement in trafficking.

I closed the site that I was on and started banging away on my keypad again. All the time, in the back of my head, I was thinking about the Wallace family, and the fact that I failed to reach out Mrs. Wallace, today.

OK, now I'm getting to the meat of things. From what I'm seeing, here, Mexico has become a major destination for sex trafficking, and a big supplier of women, to the United States. The cartel, themselves, aren't really new to the trade business, but due to their power and corrupt political connections, they're taking the business by storm. The amount of poverty, and the fact, that the victim's families, fear for their lives, also add to the cartel's success.

One thing, for sure, Mexico may be the transfer point, but women and girls are coming from all over Latin and South America, from places like, El Salvador, Columbia, and even Argentina. In some cases, poverty-stricken families are even selling young girls. What I was reading was so sad, that I wanted to cry. Don't get me wrong, Mexico doesn't actually hold the patent to this disgusting business. For example, on any given day, at ports in Los Angeles and New York, young women are being discovered on the inside of shipping containers, that started out in Asia.

For the first time, in my career, I felt defeated. I honestly don't know whether or not, I'm just spinning my wheels. I used to believe that I could clean the city streets of drugs, one community at a time, but now, the sex trade is being imported to our communities. There's a whole new battle ground, and the guy that delivers your mail, or drives a tow truck, could be part of the demand for supply!

I decided to step away from my desk, for a moment, grab a cup of coffee, and clear my mind, a little. After a few minutes away, I returned to my desk and began working on my log. It required digging up notes that I'd taken, both physical and mental. I can see now that when this case is over, I'm going to need to get away, for a while. I was so caught up in what I was doing, that when the phone on my desk rang, it startled me.

"This is Detective Cliff."

"Ricki, it's me, Captain Keller."

"So, you're checking up on me, Cap?"

"No, well, yeah, are you doing alright?"

"Not really, Captain. I've been doing some research on the trafficking of young girls, into this country."

"Don't read that crap, Detective! It's going to make you crazy!"

"Well, I have to know how these creeps, are getting these girls!"

"Detective, for all we know, they can be getting them right off the streets, of Chicago! The fact that some of them don't speak English, doesn't mean a thing. I can take you to entire communities, where not a soul speaks English!"

"Well Captain, that's not all, that I found. The DMV shows, that both, the Jaguar and TJ's Benz, are registered at the same, Country Club Hills address. Edison says, that the electric service, is billed to David Wilcox."

"What!"

"There's more, Captain. Both vehicles, are leased from a high-end dealership out in Orland Park, and guess who's footing the monthly note?"

"Don't tell me, that it's Lewis and Wilcox!"

"You've got it, Cap. I also ran a background check on Mr. Wilcox. He graduated from DePaul, majored in Criminal Justice, and minored in Immigration Law!"

"Ricki, I know where you're going with this, but it's really a stretch."

"Captain, I'm able to trace Wilcox all the way back to three years old, and then nothing. He doesn't exist, has no place of birth, and has no parents listed."

"That only means, that he was a foster kid, and I'm sure, that I don't have to tell you, that those records, are sealed."

"Well, I have one more background check, to run."

"Who are you running it on, Detective?"

"I'm running it on my big, Hispanic friend, Rafael Esteban Petreas."

"Be careful, Detective, and let me know what you find on him.

CLICK.

23

HIGHWAY TERROR

W hile I was running a background check, on Senor Petreas, a big rig truck, carrying a load of imported fruit, was pulling out of a truck stop in southern Illinois. The truck's journey had begun a day and a half ago, when it left Del Rio, Texas. It was headed north, on I-55, and being spotted by his companion, in a late model, Chevy pick-up. The sun had set, and it was beginning to get dark. It was an opportunity, for them to make a little time, or so, the drivers thought.

This part of the state is mostly corn and wheat fields. There's never a lot of traffic, and the little that there is, was slowly disappearing into small towns, housing universities. Finally, darkness had completely fallen, and the stars were out by the millions. The interstate was wide open and all theirs, with the exception of one or two trucks, headed south. The coast was clear, so the driver pushed the rig to 80 mph.

Things were going well, and they were blowing by mile markers, one, after another. Suddenly, the guys in the pick-up saw two beams of light coming from a corn field, and shining across the interstate highway. They immediately reduced their speed limit, and saw an Illinois State Trooper, come screaming out of a clearing in the fields, with its lights flashing on top of the squad car. Within seconds, he caught up with the big rig. The driver, turned on his flashers, and pulled over to the shoulder.

The trooper pulled around in front of the rig, and parked. As he was walking back to the driver's door, he paid no attention to the pick-up passing by. He had the driver step out with his driver's license and log book. After reviewing his logbook, they began walking to rear of the trailer. The trooper wanted to see that the driver was indeed, hauling what was shown on his paperwork.

The driver was getting nervous and trying, to talk the trooper out of opening the rear doors, because along with the fruit, he was carrying a very special cargo, hidden by crates of fruit, in the front of the trailer.

While all of this, was happening, the Chevy pick-up had pulled over to the shoulder, and backed all the way up to the trooper's squad car. The occupants got out, and were slowly making their way, to the rear of the trailer. By the time that they got to the rear, the large doors were open, and the trooper was inspecting the cargo. With the doors open, the trooper never saw the driver's buddies creeping up on him. Thinking that he heard something, he quickly, turned around, but it was too late! A loud bang exploded into the silent lonely stretch of highway, and the trooper fell to the ground.

He'd been shot in the head, nearly point blank. His body, was then dragged into the corn field. The rig driver then took a screw driver from the cab, and removed the license plate, revealing another, underneath it. As he was closing the rear doors, one of his buddies, drove the trooper's squad, into the field. He turned off the lights, and the engine, and then headed back to the pick-up. Moments later, both vehicles, were back on the highway, and headed north.

It was close to quitting time for me, and I was getting nowhere, fast. My background check on Petreas, showed that the Jag was registered to him, even though, he doesn't exist. How the hell, is that possible! I know that this guy didn't just fall out the sky! Despite going into the state and federal databases, there was no record of him.

Between him and Wilcox, I'm completely, baffled. One of them, doesn't exist, and the other one, just popped up, at the age of three! It's not that I'm shocked, but there's something, damn fishy, going on! As for Petreas, I don't know what I'm going to do, but I've got to find a way, to get to Wilcox's birth records. I know that the Captain wants to go by the book, so he'll be no help to me, at all.

The fact, that he wants to keep this whole mess quiet, means that there's no government agency that I can go to. Sometimes, I wonder if I'm on the wrong side of the law. In the movies, the bad guys always, have some governor in their back pocket, and they get information, like they're shopping at the dime store!

I've had enough of banging my head against the wall, for one day. I think that I'll take a ride over to Hyde Park, and have myself a Cop Special. I turned off my computer, cleaned off my desk, and was about to clock out, when my phone rang. Damn!

"This is Detective Cliff."

"Put on your damn vest, Detective!"

"Oops, you're right, Captain, I forgot."

"By the way, what did you find, on Petreas?"

"Not a damn thing! He doesn't exist! There is no record of him, being alive, state or federal."

"That's not good, Ricki!"

"You're telling me! Captain, I hate to say it, but this thing is getting worse by the minute! I can't believe, that this all started, with that little girl, lying in the burn unit, at the hospital."

"Detective, why don't you go home, and have yourself a strong one?"

"I'm way ahead of you, Cap!"

CLICK.

I hung up, and went downstairs to the locker room. I took off my blazer, strapped on my vest, and to cover it, I put on a large men's tee-shirt, that I keep just for times like these. I put my blazer back on, and took a look at myself, in the mirror. I looked just like, any other old chick, with a big stomach. Well, maybe not old, but I was ready for my Cop Special.

It took me twenty-five minutes, to make it to Hyde Park, and about five-minutes, to make it to a bar stool! This time, the bartender on duty was a petite, African American woman. She introduced herself, as Carmen.

"Hi Carman, I'm Ricki, I'm pleased to meet you."

"What can I get for you, Ricki?"

I looked around the bar, smiled, and said, that I don't see him! Carman laughed, before commenting.

"Girl, I know what you mean!"

"I'll take a cop, I mean a shot of Jack, and a draft back."

"It's coming right up, honey."

While waiting, my eyes were focused on the flat-screen TV, but my mind was worlds away. Just as Carmen was sitting my drinks down, I heard a man's voice say, put that on my tab and bring another round, for me." I turned around, to see my friend, the cop.

"Detective Little, it's good to see you!"

"It's Max, remember? Mind if I join you?"

"Please do, we can compare scars!"

"Sounds like, you had one of those days."

"That's exactly, why I'm here! This case, that I'm working on, has me climbing the walls!"

"Don't tell me, that you're still screwing around with that TJ guy!"

"Well, it turns out that he's a small fish, involved in a huge racket, and get this, the son of a bitch is protected!"

"You've got to be freaking, kidding me!"

"Apparently, he turned state's evidence on some big tuna, that the Feds wanted."

"Well, I can see why you're drinking."

"That's only the tip, of the iceberg. I've got two players who are the kingpins in this racket. One is a lawyer, that's as crocked, as a broken nose, and I can only trace him, back to three years old, which means, he's a foster kid, with sealed records. The other kingpin, is a figment of my imagination, because, state and federal records, say that he doesn't exist!"

"Maybe, you're barking up the wrong tree."

"Do you, know something, that I don't?"

"I might!"

"Well, I'm not about, to stare a gift horse, in the mouth!"

"I have to warn you. Don't get your hopes up, high. What's this lawyer's name?"

"He's Mr. David Wilcox."

"OK, got it, now how about another round?"

"Sure, but this one's on me."

24

BREAKING NEWS

After talking to Max, last night, I woke up this morning, trying to think positive. Even though he told me not to get my hopes up, I can't help it. I had exhausted all my efforts, and I was pulling out, what was left, of my hair!

I haven't forgotten about Terri, and her parents. If possible, I'd like to talk to Mrs. Wallace, today. There's still a chance of them regaining Terri's trust, and having a brighter future. For now, I'm going to have a couple of slices of toast, and a mug of coffee.

I dragged my butt out of bed, went to my small living room, and turned on the TV. I checked my phone for messages, which there weren't any, and started my coffee brewing. I took a quick shower, and twenty-five minutes later, I was sitting in my Lazy Boy, sipping coffee and watching a game show. That's when the game show was interrupted by a breaking news report.

GOOD MORNING, LADIES AND GENTLEMEN. I'M CANDEE HARRIS, COMING TO YOU LIVE FROM THE W.L.O.K. STUDIOS. THIS MORNING WE COME TO YOU, WITH HEAVY HEARTS, DUE TO THE DISCOVERY, OF THE BODY OF ONE OF OUR OWN, ILLINOIS STATE TROOPERS. RIGHT NOW, I'M GOING TO TURN THE STORY OVER TO REGINA THOMAS, WITH OUR SOUTHERN ILLINOIS AFFILIATE, W.L.P.T.

THANK YOU, CANDEE. AS CANDEE SAID, WE'RE ALL

SADDENED TO DELIVER THIS STORY TO YOU, THIS MORNING. AS YOU CAN SEE, I'M STANDING HERE, ON THIS LONELY STRETCH OF INTERSTATE 55. EARLY, THIS MORNING, THE BODY OF OFFICER ROY CLEMENS, OF THE ILLINOIS STATE TROOPERS, WAS FOUND ALONE WITH HIS SQUAD CAR.

Behind the reporter, I could see emergency personnel gathered at two separate openings in a corn field. The entire area was taped off, and the interstate was closed in both directions. Near one of the openings on the ground, was a small yellow triangle, with a number on it. The reporter was then joined by a plain clothes detective.

LADIES AND GENTLEMEN, I'VE BEEN JOINED BY DETECTIVE TONY WHITE. DETECTIVE, WHAT CAN YOU TELL US, ABOUT OFFICER CLEMENS?"

TROOPER ROY CLEMENS, WAS A SIX-YEAR VETERAN WITH THE DEPARTMENT. HE WAS OUTSTANDING AND DISTANT TO BE A LEADER, SOMEDAY. HE LEAVES BEHIND, A WIFE, AND TWO CHILDREN, 5 AND 8."

REPORTER: WHAT, IF ANYTHING, HAVE YOU BEEN ABLE TO LEARN, ABOUT THIS TRAGEDY?

FOR STARTERS, IT APPEARS TO BE A POINTLESS, EXECUTION! ACCORDING TO DISPATCH RECORDS, TROOPER CLEMENS, REQUESTED WANTS AND WARRANTS AT 8:40 PM LAST NIGHT, ON A TRACTOR-TRAILER THAT WAS EXCEEDING THE SPEED LIMIT. UNFORTUNATELY, THAT WAS THE LAST COMMUNICATION WITH HIM.

REPORTER: WAS THERE ANY EXCHANGE OF GUNFIRE BETWEEN HIM, AND HIS ASSAILANT?

TO THE BEST OF OUR KNOWLEDGE, THE SAFETY ON HIS SERVICE WEAPON WAS STILL ENGAGED, AND IT HAD NOT BEEN FIRED.

REPORTER: IS THERE ANYTHING, ON THE TRACTOR TRAILER?

THAT'S ALL THAT I CAN SAY, AT THIS TIME. THANK YOU.

With that, Detective White Stepped away.

FOLKS, WE'RE GOING TO STICK AROUND HERE, FOR A WHILE, AND AS THIS STORY UNFOLDS, WE'LL BE IN TOUCH, WITH YOU. I'M REGINA THOMAS, WITH THE W.L.P.T NEWS CREW. NOW, BACK TO CANDEE HARRIS, AT THE W.L.O.K STUDIOS, IN CHICAGO.

I turned off my set, before Miss Harris could rehash the story again. That poor guy, it sounds like he never knew it was coming. Murder seems pretty extreme, for a speeding ticket. If this were my case, the first question that I'd ask, is how in the hell, did the driver get the drop on this officer? He must've had help, and in that case, they must've been hauling one hell of a load! No legitimate courier, would kill a cop, so, that only leaves stolen property or drugs. Aside from the cop being killed, the part that I'm worried about, is the side of the interstate that was shown taped off. That side of the highway goes north, and that rig is heading our way, right now. This is just what our city needs, a truck load of trouble!

I let fifteen minutes go by, and turned my TV, back on. My game show ended, and I started getting dressed. Just as I had one pant leg on, my phone started ringing, and I damn near fell over, trying to reach it!

"Hello."

"Is this, Detective Cliff?"

"This is she."

"David Wilcox was born Jose Petreas. He's the son of a Mexican immigrant that died when he was a baby."

"What the hell! Who is this?"

"Don't worry about that! By the way, this phone is a burner, so don't waste your time!"

CLICK.

I hung up, thinking that my mystery caller, had to be Max's contact. I was so floored by the information, that I called Max, right away.

"Max, it's me, Ricki!"

"It's kind of early, for a social call, isn't it, Detective?"

"I just heard from your guy."

"What guy? I'm afraid that I don't know what, you're talking about."

"I'm sorry. Someone must be playing with my head."

CLICK.

I hung up, knowing that Max was trying to cover his ass, and now, I feel stupid! I should've known better, than to call him. I wouldn't blame him, if he never spoke to me again. As bad as I feel, the show must go on!

I guess, that it's safe to say, that David and Rafael, are family. It's not unusual, for a child to go through the foster system, and have their name, changed. Now, that I know that they're related, some other questions, may get answered, like, the cars being registered, at the same Country Club Hills address. Let's face it, if I need wheels, to get around, but I don't exist, why not, get phony identification, and register the vehicle to my brother's house.

For that matter, as far as the Benz and the Jag goes, a person, would be pretty, hard pressed, explaining how they could afford a luxury vehicle, when they haven't worked, or filed taxes, in years! Once again, blood is thicker than water. I guess, for Mr. TJ, it's just a fringe benefit!

Now I'm thinking, that if Rafael doesn't exist here in the states, there's only one other place where he can exist, and that's Mexico. The idea of these creeps being involved in trafficking, is far more believable now, that I've connected the dots. The problem is, how do I prove it, without catching them red-handed, girls and all? I decided to give Captain Keller a call.

"Good morning, Captain."

"I guess that you've seen the news, this morning."

"Oh yeah, I've seen it, alright!"

"I thought that you'd be making all kinds of speculations, about what's in the back of that truck!"

"Well, now that you've mentioned it, it's a great way to move people across the states. As long as they satisfy the guys running the scales, and do the speed limit, it should be a piece of cake! You know, Captain, I had a reason for calling, but I don't think that we should discuss it over the phone. Can we get together?"

"It's almost, lunch time. Why don't I swing by?"

"That's fine."

"Before I come, you should know, that I've received a state-wide bulletin, that hasn't been released to the media, yet. It looks like the trucker, dropped the ball!"

"What do you mean, Cap?"

"A blood stained license plate, was found in that field, not far from the body."

"Wow, that's a hell of a break!"

Hey, said the captain!

"Did you, hear that?"

"Hear what, Captain?"

"Ah, nothing, I'll tell you the rest, when I get there."

CLICK.

25

I SMELL A RAT, MAYBE TWO —————

The Captain did drop by at lunch time, and he started our conversation by saying, that he'd heard a click on the line, when we were talking earlier. If we couldn't trust anyone before, we definitely can't now! I went on, to give him all of the details, that I'd discovered, about the Petreas brothers. He was surprised, that I'd gotten the information, but didn't want to know, how, I got it. He had reached the conclusion, that we were temporarily at a standstill. Me, on the other hand, I had a plan, and that plan was to throw a monkey wrench into TJ's game, and if I'm lucky, I may flush out a couple of Vice Squad rats, at the same time! After the captain left, I started pacing, the floor. I needed the help, from one of my past clients, on the street, so to speak. He does me favors in trade, for keeping his ass, out of the joint! It was nearly 3:00 PM when I put my plan into action. As of right now, I'm waiting for the games to begin!

It was an hour, before the regular crowd, started rumbling, down the street, on their Harleys, en-route to Sally's bar. Among the crowd, was Mr. TJ, cruising in, on his Fat Boy. He didn't know it, but this was going to be a very special day, for him. As the bikers rode in, the beer was flowing, and the music was rocking. TJ stepped in feeling good, because this, was his family, and he felt right at home. He got a high five, from a couple of his buddies, and a kiss on the cheek, from one of the regular chicks, that hangout. He had regained their trust, after taking care of Tommy G., and once again, life was good.

He had downed several shots of bourbon, and was bending over the pool table, taking a shot, when he saw Rafael, walk in. He smiled at him, and Rafael winked back at him, as he headed upstairs to the office. Things were going well, and the early evening, had all the makings of a great night. As TJ made his way, around the room, the bartender, motioned to him, that he had a phone call, at the bar. He gave her the hold sign, with his forefinger.

By time he reached the bar, she had moved along to serve someone else. On the bar, the phone sat with the receiver beside it.

"Yo, what's up? This is TJ."

"Thanks, for taking my call, TJ. A couple of mutual friends told me, that you were the guy to talk to about a little private party, with some fresh honeys, from south of the border."

"Who the hell is this, and what mutual friends, are you talking about?"

"Calm down bro, they're just a couple of my boys, that have some pull, with the local department."

"Well, I don't have any freaking friends, with the local department!"

With that, TJ slammed the receiver down, on the cradle, and his mind started racing. He thought that the guys with Vice, couldn't be this stupid, but why would the guy on the phone, mention them? Seeing that he'd just gotten back in good standings, with Rafael, he knew that he'd better say something, before he found his ass on the chopping block again! Before going upstairs, he took a seat at the bar, and that's when the bartender returned.

"You look like, you've just seen a ghost!"

"Just shut up, and get me another bourbon! He was imagining how the conversation with Rafael, was going to go. He hadn't screwed up this time, but being the bearer of bad news, wasn't great either. As he sat, building up his nerves, I sat at my desk, waiting for something to happen, and something did happen. My phone rang. It was my outside help, on the street.

"So, how did it go?"

"I don't know, who this guy is, but I hope, that I never meet him, in a dark alley! He was really, pissed off!"

"Great, now stay out of trouble. I owe you one"

CLICK.

It shouldn't be long before shit, hits the fan! There's no telling what will happen, to the two Vice Squad cops. All that I can say is, that karma's a bitch! They set up Tommy G. and me, and now I've set them up. I believe that once I start breaking down the trust between these creeps, they'll start making mistakes. I don't know how, but now we've got to find that truck. How can we put a bulletin out, on a vehicle, that we can't describe? I think that I'll get the captain on the horn.

"It's me, Ricki."

"Did anything happen, that I don't want to know about?"

"Captain, I've been sitting right here at my desk, and no nothing happened, that you don't want to know about. We've got to make a decision. When will you be back, in?"

"I'm headed that way, now."

"Good, see you soon."

CLICK.

I wanted to tell the captain what I was thinking, but someone could've been listening, and I didn't want to take the risk. In the meantime, TJ had finally built up the courage, to go up the stairs, and knock on the door. Rafael opened the door, with his cellphone to his ear, and motioned to TJ to come in. He took a seat, and waited. He didn't know how the conversation started, but he listened, as Rafael spoke.

"Sí, they took out a policía. They did what they had to do, amigo!"

Rafael then looked at his watch, and said, soon. During the conversation, TJ realized that they were talking about the state trooper, that was found dead in the field. That led him to think about the shipment, coming in tonight. Everything combined, made it that much harder to tell Rafael, the bad news.

When his conversation was over, Rafael sat down at his desk and opened a drawer. From it, he removed an avocado and a large knife. He focused on slicing it open, but spoke to TJ, at the same time.

"TJ, my friend, what brings you to see an old, wetback, like me?"

"I'm sorry, but I think that I have some disturbing news."

Just like that, the big friendly grin on Rafael's face, went away.

"I thought, that you fixed that problem, my friend."

"It's not that, but I just got a strange phone call, here at the bar."

"Tell me more, about this strange phone call, my friend."

"Some guy, just told me, that he was referred to me, for a private party, with some new talent, from south, of the border."

Without saying a word, Rafael, stuck the knife, into the top of his desk, and TJ, could see his face, turning red!

"Did this gentleman, tell you who referred him, to you?"

"Well, that's the bad part, Rafael."

Rafael jumped up, and slammed his fist on the desktop! He then, took a deep breath, and relaxed.

"Now, TJ, my friend, I want you to stop, screwing around, and tell me, who has been disloyal, to our family."

"The guy said, that he was referred by a friend, that has contacts in the local department."

Rafael, immediately knew who TJ was hinting at, and went into a rage, flipping his desk over! TJ barely cleared the area, before getting his feet crushed! Rafael then placed his hands on both sides of face and yelled out!

"I knew, that I couldn't trust those bastards!"

Just about then, two huge bikers, that made TJ look like a kid, came busting into the office!

Is everything, alright, boss? asked one of them.

"Sí, now, get the hell out of here! TJ, my friend, it looks like we have rats in our house, and what do we do, when we have rats?"

"We exterminate them!"

"That's why I like you, TJ. You think like a businessman, like me."

The big, friendly grin, then returned to his face.

What about the shipment, asked TJ?

"They know about it."

Rafael, walked around the mess he'd made, and put his arm around TJ's shoulder.

"Why don't we, invite them to our little fiesta? We can make them the guest of honor! I've got a little plan for our comrades, the policía! Go downstairs, get those two goons, and bring them back up with you."

TJ left, and Rafael got on the phone to make some arrangements. His first call, was to his badge-carrying comrades. He explained, that he wanted them along for backup, maybe run a little interference, if necessary. The poor suckers, were more than happy, to join in.

He then, called the Lewis and Wilcox law firm. He told David, that there may be some changes, to the original plan, and he may, have some overnight guest, which David, didn't like at all. This was dirtier, than he wanted, to get his hands. He also, wanted an explanation, for the state trooper. Rafael, told him, that this wasn't the time, and then hung up.

TJ and the goons returned, and the evening's events were discussed. One of the changes, was the addition of an extra big-rig. If things go as planned, it will be used as a decoy, to lure the two Vice Squad cops.

There was nothing special about my own plan, to get these two cops, out of my hair. I was just taking a shot in the dark, and hoping that TJ would panic. The one thing which really worked in my favor, was the fact, that no one likes dirty cops, no matter what side of the fence, that they're on. Sooner or later, Rafael, was going to get bored with these two, anyway, and that's when they were going to disappear!

26

FUN WITH THE FEDS

I wanted to have all of my ducks in a row, when the Captain walked in. I hadn't come up with a possible solution, for locating the big-rig, so I figured, that I'd try digging a little deeper, into the subject of the Cartel, by reaching out to Chicago's division of the Federal Bureau of Investigations. Their line rang twice, before I got a male voice that was polished, and sounded like he was reading a script.

"You've reached the Federal Bureau of Investigations. I'm Special Agent Collins. Is this an emergency?"

"No sir, it's not. I'm Detective Ricki Cliff, with the Chicago Police Department."

"How may I help you, Detective?"

"Well, actually, I only have one question. Is there a cartel, by the name of Petreas, currently operating south of the border?"

"Hold on, Detective, I'll have to transfer you, but first, I'll need your badge number."

It was obvious, that I'd really freaked this guy out! I gave him my badge number, and waited for what felt like, forever. Finally, another mechanical voice, got on the line.

"Good afternoon. Detective Cliff, is it?"

He continued speaking before I could answer him, and I could tell, that this wasn't going to go too far.

"If you don't mind me asking, Detective, what is your interest in the cartel?"

"I'm just trying to get a simple answer, to a simple question."

"Well, Detective, I'm afraid that the Bureau doesn't have access to that kind of information."

"I knew that I could count on you guys! Have a good day!"

CLICK.

What a bunch of crap! The effort which he put into trying to avoid the subject, answered my question. Thank God, that those guys have a desk job, because they'd be lost, on the streets!

"So, you're talking to yourself now, Detective?"

I must've been thinking out loud, when the Captain walked up, behind me.

"Do you want to have a seat here, or do you want to go into your office?"

"We'd better go into my office. What were you mumbling, about?"

"Oh, that! I'll tell you, in your office."

I followed the captain, and he closed the door, behind us.

"Captain, when you walked in, I had just gotten off the horn, with the Feds."

"The Feds? What made you turn to those guys?"

"I was trying to get confirmation, that a Petreas Cartel actually, exists."

"Jesus, Ricki, do you know, what you just did?"

"Relax, Captain! They didn't help me, well, not directly. They claimed that they don't have access to that kind of information. What a crock!"

"You don't get it, do you, Detective?"

"Get what?"

"If they didn't want you dead, before, you can damn bet, that they do now! Did you forget about the phones?"

"Ah damn! That's right!"

"Do you have anything else, Detective?"

"I gave up at first, but I now think that there may be a way of locating that truck."

"Detective, I'm all for nailing the guy that killed that trooper, but are we sure, that the truck is priority, right now?"

"We have the fingerprints, and the possibility, that the trooper was killed because of the cargo. Not only that, but the Feds damn near admitted, that the Petreas Cartel does exist! I think that's more than enough reason, to make this priority. Do you want to hear, my idea?"

"Sure, why not?"

"For starters, we need to verify what state that license plate is from, if it was stolen or not, and if it was used long enough, to make it to our state. When that rig entered southern Illinois, it crossed the scales, somewhere."

"That's right, and there should be surveillance footage, showing the truck. We'd better get on it right away, because they'll be pulling in here sometime, tonight. That is, if they're coming to Chicago."

"One more thing, Cap. I think that we should limit this information, to the Illinois State Troopers only."

"That's a good idea, not to mention, that that truck can't be driven on most city streets."

The Captain went downstairs to use the desk sergeant's phone, and I went back to my desk. On my computer, I searched for the address and phone numbers of weight stations, between southern Illinois and Chicago. After taking note of all of them, I turned to go back to the captain's office, and that's when my phone rang.

"This is Detective Cliff."

"Good evening, Detective. Please, don't say my name! I just collared a guy, that hangs out at a strangely popular bar, and he wants to cut a deal, by giving up current information, that you should hear."

"Really? Let's have it!"

"According to this guy, a contract hit, has been put out on your life, and he's scared to death, to say, who ordered it. I've got to go."

CLICK.

I hung up, and wrapped by arms around my rips, a knee jerk reaction, to checking for my vest. The incident on my bike, was one thing, but if a bounty, was offered to Sally's general public, that's a whole different, freaking thing!

I've been cut, stabbed, and shot at, but never, have I not known, who my opponent was, or what direction, he was coming from. I'm afraid, to tell, the captain, because he might, pull me, off the case, completely. I sat at my desk, in a complete daze, wondering, what to do.

"Ricki, Ricki, Detective!"

I jumped, because he startled me!

"What's going on, with you? You look like, you just lost your best friend, or something!"

"Captain, I have something to say, but you've got to make me a promise, first."

"Detective, you know me well enough, to know, that I'm not making you any damn promises, especially, if it has anything to do, with me, taking you off of this case!"

"Cap, I really need your trust, and support, on this."

"Ricki, you're a great cop, but you do so many things, off the books, and against the grain, that you make trust, be a challenge for me. Now, spit it out!"

"I just received a phone call, from an unknown person."

"So, this is how, you ask for my trust, by not telling me, who it was from?"

OK Cap, he's a cop, a good cop, and I don't want his name, dragged into this."

"So, what did, this so-called, good cop, have to say?"

"He collared a guy this evening, that wanted to cut a deal, for some information. There's been a contract, put out on my life. Evidently, there was an open offer, made at Sally's bar. OK, now you know."

"I have one question for you, Detective. Tell me why, I shouldn't pull your ass, off this case, right now?"

"Do you really, want a reason, really, Captain? I'll tell you why! First of all, you wouldn't know jack about these guys, if it weren't for me! Second of all, no one cares about these kids, like I do, and taking me off of this case, won't take the contract, off my ass, as you put it!"

"You know, Detective, you take, the damn cake! I can't live with you, and I can't live, without you!"

27

THE RIDE HOME

I guess that I had blown the captain away, by standing up for myself. I just told the truth. I admit that I bend the rules sometimes, or actually break a few, but hell, I'm out there by myself, and I do what I have to do! As of right now, I'm back at my desk, staring at the clock, and the Captain's, in his office. I don't think that he's real big on replacing me, because then he'd have to explain where and how, information was obtained. Having a rebel on his squad, is a reflection of his leadership, as well.

In the meantime, our northbound big-rig and the Chevy pick-up, have merged from I-55 to the Tri-State Tollway. Following directions from their G.P.S., they were headed for a truck stop, right outside of the town of Elmhurst, Illinois. After pulling off the road, into the truck stop, they drove slowly through the parking area. At the far end, they found one lonely rig sitting, parked beside it, and waited. The pick-up parked 6 or 7 spaces to the side of them.

The passenger in the pick-up, got on his phone, and called Rafael, to inform him that they were in position. Rafael then called his buddies from the Vice Squad, to have them meet him out at the truck stop. He left his office, and as he was walking through Sally's, he gave TJ the signal. TJ gave him a half-hour lead, and then he and four of his biker buddies, headed out on their Harleys. They had a plan, and it included returning without two of the party-goers!

Finally, the captain stepped out his office, and came over to my desk.

"We got lucky, and got a hit on the big-rig. A photo of the cab with the serial numbers, and the trailer, has been fed to every onboard computer, in each of the trooper's squads. It's now just a matter of time. Why don't you, go on home?"

"That's good news, Captain."

I kind of, had mixed emotions. It's not, that I felt bad about things, but I understand the position, that he's in.

"Captain, there's one more thing. Are we, alright?"

"Honestly, I thought about it, but I really, have no choice, and when this is all over, we're going to have to sit down, and talk. Now go home. I'll keep you posted."

My shift wasn't quite over yet, but I took off like the Captain suggested. I really couldn't wait to get home. I needed the alone time. I thought about going over to Hyde Park, but I really wasn't in the mood, for being around happy people, nor did I want to bring anyone down, so I stopped at the liquor store, on my way home. After purchasing a bottle of Jack and a bag of chips, I said good night to the clerk and went back out, to my bike.

I secured my package to the rear of my seat with some elastic netting, and put my helmet on. Just as I was swinging my leg over, to get on, I saw a flash from across the street, and something hit me so hard in my ribs, that it knocked me off my bike! The feeling of severe pain, and agony, immediately set in! On the ground now, I began squirming and screaming! The point of impact, felt like, it was on fire and my rips felt like, they had exploded! As I lay on the sidewalk, with tears being forced out of my eyes, I heard a car, burning rubber and leaving the scene! The pain was horrible, and getting worse by the second! My breathing had increased to an out-of-control rhythm. At the moment, I had no idea of what had happened, to me. All that I know is, that the store clerk appeared, kneeling down over me. Not being able to stop moving, I screamed at him!

"I'm a cop! Call 911"

I kept reaching around, and touching myself, feeling and looking for blood or anything! As the clerk ran back inside, to call 911, a crowd started gathering. I then began feeling vulnerable, because God knows, who could've walked up and finished me off! The only thing that I wanted to go away more than the pain, was the crowd! I was trying to sit up when I heard a siren approaching in the distance. My sense of timing, connection with reality, and my nerves, were all twisted. The next sound that I heard, was that of a woman's voice, which I recognized.

138

"Alright, clear the way! Coming through! Back up!"

Though my vision was a bit fuzzy, I could see that it was the young female uniform, who dropped me off at home, before. I had forgotten her name, and we both were surprised to see each other. She knelt down, over me.

"Detective, what the hell happened, to you?"

I was still a little hysterical, and when I told her that I was getting on my bike, and that's when she interrupted me.

"That's your bike?"

She then lifted up my tee-shirt, and saw that I was wearing a vest. Trying to be gentle, she slowly pulled back the Velcro straps. As hard as she tried, it still hurt like hell, and I screamed again! She separated the front and back panels, to take a look. That's when her eyes, got real big!

"Detective, I believe that you've been shot!"

Moaning, I told her to take a look at my vest. Sure enough, she found a smashed-up slug, still in it. Just about then, the EMTs showed up. After being examined, it was confirmed that I had been shot. Thanks to my vest, the results were bruised ribs, and a shit load of pain! I wanted to get on my bike and ride home, but it was nearly impossible to stand up, let alone, get back on my bike. My young friend, had the police pound pick it up, for me.

The EMTs wanted to take me to the hospital, for X-rays and further examination, but I refused to ride with them. Instead, I had the young uniform, take me in. While I was being treated at the hospital, the Captain showed up.

"What the hell, happened to you, Detective? I thought that you were going home!"

He then stopped yelling, and looked at the young officer.

"Oh I'm sorry, I'm Captain Keller. How did you happen to come across, Detective Cliff?"

"I was just out on patrol, and saw a crowd building across the street, at the liquor store, and there she was, Sir."

"Well, I've got it from here. Thank you, Officer."

Take care, Detective, said the young officer, before walking away.

She left the room, and the captain, gave me one of his looks!

"So, I guess that the rumor of the contract, has been confirmed!"

Before I could comment, the young officer returned to my room.

"Sorry, but I forgot about this. I took it off your back seat. I thought that you might need it. Good night."

She sat the bag on the nightstand and took off.

"Captain, I just want to go home! The doctor can write me a prescription, and I can get the hell out of here! There's nothing else that they can do, for me."

"Why do I feel like it's going to be a waste of my time, to argue with you?" Even if I put my foot down, I still imagine you going over the wall, using bed sheets, as a damn rope!"

"Captain, you've been watching too many movies, and if it makes you feel any better, it hurts like hell!"

"You know, Ricki. It's alright to be scared. It's just me and you, not those jerks in the squad room."

"I know Captain, but what I really want is my…"

"Let me guess, your damn bike!"

"Well, that too, but I want to pick-up a Vicki from the Motor Pool, tomorrow."

"Are you crazy? Never mind, don't answer that! I'm not even, going to worry about it, because I don't believe, that you'll be able to climb out of bed, in the morning. For God's sake, Ricki, you've been shot! Let me find a doctor, so I can get you home."

"Hey Cap, I love you too."

"Yeah, don't push it!"

28

REHABILITATION

Against the recommendation of the doctor, Captain Keller managed to spring me from the hospital, along with a prescription for Vicodin. After driving through an all-night pharmacy, he took me home, and helped me get comfortable on my sofa. Before leaving, I had him pour me a glass of water, and a glass of my Jack. He then took off and I turned on the TV.

A late-night talk show was on, which was fine with me, because I needed a laugh, even though it hurt to do it. The guest included, a pro football player, that looked as sculpted as the Atlas Statue, and a beautiful young Country Western singer, that was supposed to be currently, high on the charts, both of whom, I'd never heard of.

Just as I was getting into the career lifestyles of these two, the picture changed to the scene of my liquor store, and the words BREAKING NEWS rolled across the screen. That prompted me to take a swallow of my Jack! Once again, private owned, police band scanners, had struck! With nothing else going on this time of night, the local media jumped all over this story. The reporter wasted no time, in getting to the heart of things.

GOOD EVENING, LADIES AND GENTLEMEN. WE'RE COMING TO YOU LIVE, FROM OUTSIDE OF ED'S LIQUOR MART, WHERE EARLIER TONIGHT, WAS THE SCENE OF AN ATTEMPT MADE ON THE LIFE OF ONE OF CHICAGO'S FINEST!

I thought to myself, wow! I've been upgraded to finest! It seemed like it was just yesterday, that I was the local slut, who was sleeping with Councilman Lee! Well, that's the media for you. One day, they hate you, and the next day, they love you!

THAT'S RIGHT, FOLKS. CHICAGO POLICE DETECTIVE, RICKI CLIFF, WAS SHOT, WHEN SHE STEPPED OUT OF THIS STORE, AFTER MAKING A PURCHASE. OUR SOURCES TELL US, THAT SHE WAS OFF DUTY AT THE TIME OF THE SHOOTING, BUT STRANGELY ENOUGH, SHE WAS WEARING A BULLET PROOF VEST. WITHOUT A DOUBT, THAT VEST SAVED HER LIFE, BUT THE QUESTION REMAINS, WHY WAS SHE WEARING IT, IF SHE WAS OFF DUTY? COULD IT BE, THAT THIS WASN'T A RANDOM ATTEMPT ON HER LIFE? COULD THERE BE MORE TO THIS STORY? WE'LL STAY ON TOP OF THIS ONE! NOW, BACK TO OUR REGULAR SCHEDULED PROGRAM.

Great, that's just what I needed, more damn advertisement! Why don't they just paint a damn bull's eye on my back! I was just about ready for my first, in a series of Vicodin, that I'd be taking, when my phone rang. I was wondering, who in the hell, can it be!

"Yeah, this is Cliff!"

"I see that you made the celebrity list, again, Detective!"

"Hey Max, I guess that you think that I'm dumb as a bag of rocks!"

"No Ricki, not at all, it could've happened to anyone. The good thing is, that you were smart enough, to wear a vest."

"Well, you know, that I can't go into detail, on this phone, but this thing, is huge! I'm nothing, but a bump on the road, to these people, and the fact, that they keep coming after me, proves that they're going ahead, with their plans. I'm telling you Max, something big, is about to go down, in this city!"

"Wait a minute! What do you mean, they keep coming, after you?"

"A few days ago, there was a story in the news about three bikers, that went down in an accident. Two died at the scene, and one's a vegetable."

"Yeah, I hurt about that."

"Well Max, I was on my bike, and they tried to spread me, across the pavement, only things, didn't quite, go that way!"

"For crying out loud, Ricki, you don't need a bulletproof vest, you need a freaking Sherman Tank! Whoever these people are, they're using these bikers to do their dirty work, and those guys multiply like freaking cock roaches! So, what's your next plan?"

"Seeing that I won't be climbing back on my bike for a while, my next move, is picking up a Vicki, from the Motor Pool, tomorrow. As for right now, I'm about to pass out from Jack Daniels and Vicodin."

"Well honey, you get all the rest that you can, and don't be in such a hurry, to get behind the wheel."

"I'll take that into consideration, Max. Good night."

CLICK.

I turned off the TV, and got as comfortable as I could, on my sofa, and soon I was out, like a light!

Out at the truck stop, Rafael's plan was in progress, and he was giving out commands, like a four-star general. The driver of the big rig, that was sitting parked, when his guys showed up, was inside the cab, sleep. The poor guy, had no idea, of what was about to unfold, right outside his door. He was awakened, by the sound of a pistol butt, knocking on his window.

Startled and afraid for his life, he didn't bother to put up a fight. After climbing out of his cab, he was forced to open the doors of his trailer, and that's when he began to plead.

"Please, please, take what you want, but don't kill me, I have a family!"

That gave Rafael an idea, and he grabbed the guy by his forearm and turned him around to face him.

Give me your driver's license, said Rafael.

Taking a look around, to make sure that they were alone, he ordered the girls, to be transferred to the open trailer. Once, that they were loaded, and the doors of the trailer, were secured, one of Rafael's men, climbed into the cab, fired it up, and headed for the next transfer point. Again, the driver started freaking out, and asking questions.

"What are you going to do, to me? Please, don't hurt me!"

Rafael looked at him, with the eyes of the Devil, himself! He then, gave another command.

"Take him and put him behind the wheel of our rig. If he makes a move, shut him!"

At the far end of the parking lot, a set of headlights appeared, and they all drew their weapons. Soon, the headlights blinked. It was the two Vice Squad cops. They were focused on the gathering at the big-rig. Behind them, TJ and his biker brothers were just arriving, but it didn't bother the two cops, one bit. The officers got out of their unmarked squad car, and approached the rear of the trailer. Right away, by the look in Rafael's eyes, they knew that something was up! When they found themselves surrounded by TJ and his boys, three of which, holding bats, their suspicions were confirmed, and one of the cops yelled out!

"What the hell, is going on, here?"

He got his answer, when he felt the crushing blow of a baseball bat, making contact with his knee cap! He fell to the ground, and his partner drew his service weapon, but he was too late! TJ stepped up behind him, and put the barrel of his pistol to the back of his head. That's when Rafael spoke up.

"I'm sorry amigos, but you talk too much, for Rafael!"

He then gave the signal, and the beating commenced.

The driver was sitting in the rig, at gunpoint, and was scared to death, as he listened to the screams and moans of the two cops. During the beating, one of the cops managed to pull his pistol out, but it was quickly kicked out of his hand and TJ put a round in his chest! His partner was beaten nearly to death, and the two of them were dragged and set inside the trailer of the rig. Inside, they were cuffed together, with their own handcuffs.

The doors were closed and locked. With the exception of Rafael and the driver of the pick-up truck, everyone else, took off. Rafael walked up to the door of the cab and opened it. The driver was shaking like a leaf! Rafael held his driver's license up, looked at it, and in his strong Hispanic voice, he spoke to the driver.

"This is what you're going to do, my friend. You're going to drive this rig back out, on the highway, and head north."

He then, took another look at the license, and showed it to the driver.

"We've got G.P.S., on this rig, and if it stops, or gets off the highway, we're going to pay a little visit to your family! Do you understand, amigo?"

The guy was so afraid, that he couldn't speak. Rafael's man climbed out of the cab, and the guy fired it up. The two of them then stood, watching, as the rig pulled out of the truck stop, and got on the ramp, leading to the highway. They then followed the rig for about a mile, before getting off of the tollway.

29

I NEED HELP ⟋

After a drug induced night of rest, I woke up, not remembering the events of last night, until I tried to sit up. I instantly got flashbacks, of the entire incident. Although it was truly painful, I managed to get up and make it to the shower. Normally, taking a shower is one of my favorite activities. I can stand and let the water beat on my back forever. That was not the case, this morning, however! Among other things, the bandages around my ribs were an issue.

Lifting my arms in the air was nearly impossible, and I gave up twice on getting dressed. Finally, I admitted to myself, that I was going to need help. I thought about my neighbor, across the hall, and even though she's sweet, she's also a bit too nosy, and I can't handle that right now. I also thought about Max, but it would be inappropriate, not to mention, that I just met the guy.

I decided to call my buddy, the desk sergeant, at the precinct. I had to remind him of the young female officer, that arrived at the scene, last night. I still couldn't remember her name, and after a couple of minutes of trial and error, he found records of her dropping me off, the first day that I met her.

"I've got it, Detective. She's Officer Linda McCoy."

"Great, now give me her phone number."

"I don't know about that, Detective."

"Come on, Sarge! It's a female thing! You're not going to make me explain it to you, are you?"

"OK Ricki, but you didn't get it, from me!"

"Thanks, Sarge, I love you!"

I hung up, thinking Linda McCoy, Linda McCoy. I never want to forget that name again. It was beginning, to get embarrassing. I logged Linda's number into my phone, and then gave her a call.

"Good morning, who's calling?"

"Good morning, Linda. It's Detective Cliff. I hope that I didn't wake you."

"Detective, how are you doing, this morning?"

"Well, that's kind of why I'm calling. I'm dealing with the pain, but getting dressed, is impossible."

"Do you need some help, Detective?"

"I'm so embarrassed!"

"Don't be. My shift doesn't start for a few hours. Why don't you relax, and give me about twenty-five minutes?"

"Thank you so much, Officer, I mean, Linda!"

CLICK.

While waiting for Officer McCoy to arrive, I put on a pot of coffee. Trying to limit my movements, I unlocked my apartment door, called Linda back, and gave her the lobby door code, for downstairs. Before getting comfortable, I put my pistol under a pillow, near me on the sofa. After last night, who knows what kind of slime may be lurking around, my place! In any case, I'm ready to go down with my boots on. Well, in this case, that'll be my slippers!

Thirty minutes later, there was a soft knock at my door. I drew my weapon, pointed it at the door, and said, come in. Linda stepped in and immediately raised her arms, trying to shield her body.

"Whoa! Detective, it's me!"

"Sorry, Linda, but these days, I have to, well, you know! Please, come on in, there's a fresh pot of coffee in the kitchen."

She came in, locked the door, and then headed for my small kitchen. She prepared two mugs of coffee, and joined me on the sofa.

"Are you sure, that you're up for this, Detective? Maybe, you should spend a day on the sofa."

"Yeah, I'm up for it, plus, I have things to do, and by the way, it's Ricki, from now on."

"Well, as long as we're on a first name basis, can I ask you a question?"

"Sure, go for it, honey."

"Is it true, what I've heard?"

"Knowing me, there's a damn good chance, that it is!"

"I hear, that there's a contract hit, out on you. Please tell me, that it's not true!"

"Sorry honey, but it's true."

At first, Linda just looked at me, and then she snapped out of it.

"Well, are you ready for this, Ricki?"

"As ready, as I'll ever be!"

We entered my bedroom, and Linda started laughing. What's so damn funny, I asked. She pointed at all the clothes spread out on the floor around my bed.

"It looks like you had quite a battle, and lost!"

I couldn't help but join her in the laughter, but even that hurt.

"First, let's get you undressed, Ricki."

One thing, that I can say for this kid, there's not a shy bone in her body! On the floor, were the panties, that I failed putting on earlier. She spread them out on the floor, so that I could step into the openings. Slowly, and gently, she slipped them over my feet, and up my legs to my thighs. She then untied my bath robe, and pulled the panties over my ass, as I took a deep breath.

"OK, Ricki, I know that was a bit, painful, so let's take a breather, for a moment."

In my mind, I was thinking, that I needed a breather, more than she knew!

"Ricki, is there any chance, that you have a sports bra? Because the straps on this one, is going to irritate you, all day."

As she stood there, holding my bra, I was amazed by how much she cared about the pain, that I was in.

"Yeah, take a look in the top drawer. At this point, I don't care about the color."

She pulled open the drawer and froze, just staring down into it. Then it hit me! I'd forgotten, that that's where I keep mommy's little helper! I was too embarrassed to say anything, so I acted as if, I didn't notice. Moments later, she reached in, and pulled out one of my sports bras.

"How's this one, Ricki?"

This time, the look in her eyes was different, and I was thinking that now, the shoe was on the other foot, because she was the one, that looked embarrassed.

"OK, Ricki, take a deep breath, and I'm just, going to go for it!"

I began to moan and scream all at once. I couldn't help myself! It was like being shot all over again, and it even brought tears to my eyes! The whole time, Linda kept saying how sorry she was. Finally, the torture was over, and she wiped the tears from my cheeks, with her thumbs. Smiling, she looked at me.

"We did it, Ricki! Now, let's just relax, until you get your strength back. How about another mug of coffee?"

"I've got a better idea! There's a bottle of Jack in the kitchen. Why don't you pour me a shot?"

I was sitting on my bed, when I heard my cellphone ring in the living room. I called out to Linda and told her to answer it. I then slowly got up, and made my way to the living room.

"Cliff residence, this is Officer McCoy, speaking."

"This is Captain Keller. What are you doing there, Officer?"

Linda mouthed Captain Keller, to me.

"Detective Cliff needed a little female help, this morning, Sir. Can you hold, a moment?"

She handed me the phone, and placed the shot of Jack on the cocktail table.

"Good morning, Captain."

"How is my little, super woman, this morning?"

"She's not feeling too super, but thanks for the compliment!"

"I've got some incredible news for you, but it has to be quick! I'm in Elmhurst, at a truck stop. We've found the Vicki belonging to the two Vice officers. There's evidence that they may've been killed. You'd better turn on your TV set. I've got to go!"

CLICK.

I quickly pointed at the remote, and Linda turned on the TV set. The morning's programs were already interrupted, and the truck stop, off the tollway, was being shown. There was law enforcement all over the place, including Captain Keller. In the background, we could see the beginnings of a total media circus, going on! That's when I asked Linda if she had her gear with her.

"I always keep my badge and service weapon, with me."

"Good, now, help me into my vest!"

30

YOU REAP, WHAT YOU SOW

I needed Linda to chauffeur me around a bit. I knew that I was asking for a lot, during her time off, but I really wanted to be out at the scene. It was still mid-morning, and she didn't mind, but boy, that I get a surprise when we got downstairs, to her car. I took one look at it, and pain was written all over my face, because it was a VW bug!

"Honey, I love you for doing this, but we've got to stop by Motor Pool, and pick up a Vicki!"

"Yeah, I know that it's a little difficult, getting in and out of it, plus the Vicki will give you a chance to take a crack behind the wheel, on our way back."

After being shoehorned into her car, it took us about twenty minutes to get to the station. As it turns out, she had quite the lead foot, which was fine with me. Once, that we had switched vehicles, I felt like, I was riding in a stretch limo. As soon, as we got on the Tri-State Tollway, we hit the lights and siren. Again, her lead foot came in handy.

When we arrived, there were even more cops and media present, than what we'd seen on the TV. One block before the entrance, to the truck stop, orange cones had been setup to redirect traffic, past the truck stop. At the entrance, I flashed my badge at the trooper on duty. There were several other big-rigs parked, but not ours. At the cab of each one, a driver was being interviewed by a State Trooper.

Due to the number of law enforcement vehicles present, we couldn't get very close, to the infamous dark blue Ford Victoria. We had to walk a good thirty yards to reach the vehicle. As we approached it, I got

153

flashbacks of the first time that I saw it, turning the corner. It appeared to be completely untouched. Nothing had taken place, at the vehicle.

The poor bastards must've thought that everything was alright and walked right into hell! The million-dollar question is, where the hell are the two cops? Sitting a couple of car lengths ahead of the Vicki, was a tow truck, waiting for orders to tow it away. Up ahead, we saw Captain Keller with some other officers. They were near the taped-off area, looking down at the ground.

Finally, we reached him, and he turned around, to greet us. I was waiting for him to chew me out, for being there, especially with an off-duty officer.

"There's no truck, and no girls, Ricki. Come with me and let me show you what we've got."

Linda then, gave me, a funny look.

"What girls, is he talking about?"

"You don't want to get involved in this, honey! It'll come out in the end, don't worry."

The captain showed us a clear, plastic evidence bag, containing a semiautomatic pistol, that had already been traced back to one of the Vice cops. In the middle of the taped-off area, was a pool of dry blood and it appeared that at least one person had been dragged through it, away from the area. The trail ended at the edge of a parking space.

"Is there a camera around here, Cap?"

"I'm a step ahead of you, Detective, and by the way, what the hell, are you two doing here, anyway?"

"Oh, well I thought that...

"Yeah, I know what you thought, Ricki! Officer McCoy, whatever you do, don't let the detective's bad habits rub off on you!"

"Captain, I knew, that Rafael would turn against these two cops."

"Yeah well, when you play with the Devil, you get burned! As long as we're on the subject, what exactly did you do to Rafael, to make him turn against them?"

"Actually, it wasn't Rafael, it was TJ."

Before I could give the captain the details, we were interrupted by a young state trooper.

"Excuse me, Captain Keller?"

"Yes, how can I help you?"

"Captain, one of our guys was just waved down by a guy walking along the tollway. He claims that he was taken at gunpoint last night, and was forced to drive a big-rig, that wasn't his."

"What! Did he say where, he left the rig?"

"He's in the back seat of one our squads, right now, Sir."

"Thanks, Officer. Come on, ladies!"

"Sir, there's one more thing that you should know. These people know where he lives, and they've threatened to kill his family, if he says anything."

"Jesus Christ, those bastards!"

The three of us, all got into the captain's squad. While he maneuvered through the different law enforcement vehicles, I got on the radio to get the location, of the missing big-rig. We were in luck. The driver had left it, just twenty miles north of where we were. He saw that the coast was clear and jumped out, at a lonely stretch of highway.

I hated, to ask the captain, but I had to.

"Cap, do you think that those guys may have someone watching that truck, and ready to go ahead with their threat, to this man's family?"

"I don't want to believe that Detective, but I wouldn't put it past those jerks! You'd better get on the horn and get a detail over to this guy's home, right away. I want his family out of that house, now!"

Once again, we got lucky. The driver drove a local route, and his house was within reach of the Chicago P.D. At the speed that we were driving, it didn't take long, to get to the abandoned big-rig. When we arrived, the state troopers already had both sides of the tollway closed down. The rig was surrounded by squads, but no one, had approached it yet. They were waiting for Captain Keller's arrival.

The local fire department paramedics were on hand as well, in hopes that the two vice cops were inside the rig, and alive. As of right now, no one other than the captain and me, are aware of the theory that the girls may be inside, also. This could be an eye opener, for all involved.

The Captain slammed on the breaks right beside another squad. When he did it, the automatic seat-belt tightened around my body. Again, I endured the feeling of being shot once more! I had no choice but to scream. Sorry, said the Captain.

"You should've stayed home!"

"Did I tell you today that I love you, Captain?"

"No, you didn't!"

"Good!"

Three of us, plus two troopers, approached the rig's rear doors, with our weapons drawn. The captain and one of the officers, holstered their weapons, and grabbed the latch on each door. We all froze, and lowered our weapons, when we saw the contents. There, sitting back-to-back with their hands cuffed together, were our missing vice cops. It was obvious that they both had expired, hours ago. One was sitting in a puddle of his own, dried-up blood, with his eyes, still open. Following protocol, the Captain had the paramedics come over and check their vital signs.

The three of us stepped back, as the troopers climbed up inside the trailer. Careful not to contaminate any of the evidence, around the two dead officers, they combed the entire trailer. As we stood waiting, I noticed that one of the vice cops still had his weapon holstered. If it weren't for these two trying to get me killed, I'd almost feel sorry for them.

One of the troopers walked back toward us, with the strangest look on his face. I could see that he was holding something, but I didn't know what it was.

"Detectives, you're not going to believe what I've just found, in here!"

In one hand, he held old wrappers from food items, and in the other hand, he held a box of feminine hygiene products. The captain and I both looked at each other, and then the trooper spoke again.

"Why the hell, would this kind of stuff be in there?"

It hit the captain and me at the same time, and we both said the same thing, at the same time.

THEY PULLED A SWITCH!

The driver! The Captain said

"They're in his truck!"

He ran over to the squad, where the driver was still sitting in the back seat. The trooper then asked me, what kind of switch, are we talking about?

"We'll fill you in later, but first, we've got to find that guy's truck!"

The Captain got the truck description, plate, and serial numbers, and immediately requested that an all-points bulletin, be put out on the truck. We were getting closer, I could feel it! I got a call from the desk sergeant, and he informed me, that the driver's wife and kids were sitting comfortably, in our station. The wife was a nervous wreck, but safe and dying to see him. I went over to the squad, to tell him in person.

"Hi, I'm Detective Cliff, what's yours?"

"My friends call me Jimbo."

"Well Jimbo, I've got good news for you! Your wife and children are safe and sound. Right now, they're at the police station. As soon as we can, we're going to take you to them."

The poor guy, was so overcome with emotion, that a couple of tears, ran down his cheeks. I then motioned for Linda, to join us.

"Jimbo, this is Officer McCoy. She's going to keep you company, while I go and see about getting you out of here."

When I turned, to walk away, Linda was already starting a calming conversation with him. I knew that we wouldn't find that big-rig in a heartbeat, plus it wouldn't be long, before Linda had to start her real shift. There wasn't much that we could do, on this stretch of highway. I told the Captain that I wanted to get Jimbo to his family, as well as get Linda to the precinct.

He suggested that we get one of the troopers to take us back to the truck stop and our unmarked squad. The coroner arrived, and the Captain was going to stay and see this thing out. I turned to leave, and he called back.

"You've got good instincts, Detective. It's not over yet, but you did well. I hate to say it, but don't get your hopes up regarding the cartel. If we nail this bunch alone, we've done the world a favor! You've done enough for one day. Why don't you take the rest of the day off and give those ribs a rest?"

"Thanks, Captain."

31

DOWNTIME

Aside from my injury, I felt pretty good during the ride home. We had made some accomplishments in this case, and we were about to reunite a man with his family, who thought that he'd never see them again. It was a bummer to have to break the news to him, that he and his family wouldn't be going home. To be on the safe side, the city is going to place them in a secured hotel. At least they'll be together and safe.

When we got back to the station, Linda went straight to her car to retrieve a duffle bag. I thanked her for everything and told her that I owe her. I took Jimbo to a room that is set up like a lounge. We keep it available, so that grieving families can have privacy. As soon as I opened the door, his family came running toward him. It was a very touching moment, so I left them alone.

After completing some paperwork, I introduced Jimbo and his family to the officer that would pick up, where I left off. I said goodbye, and prepared myself for one more task, which was getting behind the wheel of a Vicki. So far today, I had gotten in and out of vehicles, at least six times, and I had that part, down pat. The real challenge, is going to be turning the wheel. I went out to the Vicki, opened the passenger door, and laid my sidearm on the seat. After walking around to the driver's side, I eased onto the seat and said, to hell with the seat-belt! After getting squared away, I took a moment to collect my thoughts.

The drive home wasn't fun, but it was tolerable. The first thing I did when I got home, was to gather up all of my vices and put them on the cocktail table, so that they'd be in reach. Once I had my pillows all fluffed up and ready, I grabbed the remote and eased back on the sofa.

I turned on the TV, only to find that the media had left the scene of the abandoned squad car, and relocated to the discovery location of the bodies, out on the Tri-state. The story had gotten huge, and the media doubled too! No matter what station I turned to, the on-the-spot reporter had his or hers spill on the circumstances, regarding the slain officers. It was incredible! I wonder if they teach these guys that crap or are they all graduates from the University of Dr. Seuss! Man, if I could do that, I'd solve every crime in the city, in one week!

After about forty minutes, I dozed off and a couple of hours later, I woke to the sound of my phone. It was the Captain calling.

"Hey, Cap."

"I've got some semi-good news for you. The surveillance camera out at the truck stop, caught the assault on the two officers. The fact that it was dark out, made it kind of grainy, but our lab boys worked with it, and we've got a fairly decent photo of TJ. He was the trigger man, and this time, the Feds won't be able to save his ass! There's already a bulletin out on him, and he'll never make it out of the state. In addition to that, I'm organizing an early morning raid at the house, where you saw those girls. Even if he's not there, we'll get those girls off the streets, and back to their families."

"That's great news, Captain! What about Mr. Rafael?"

"Unfortunately, his back was to the camera, but the truck driver can identify him, not only that, but he witnessed the transfer of the girls, from trailer to trailer."

"Did he see the assault, on the cops?"

"No, they had forced him into the cab before then, but he did hear it, and that's what freaked him out, the most."

"Captain, this guy is a huge witness, and you know what that means!"

"Yeah, if he testifies against Rafael, there's a good chance, that the cartel may come after him."

"The worst part is, that the cartel, has longer arms than law!"

"Well, there's always the relocation program."

"That's easy for you and I to say, because we see it all the time! Jesus, Captain! That poor guy! Why is it that I suddenly feel like crap, for doing the right thing?"

"Yeah, I know the feeling."

"I guess that there's no word on the truck, yet?"

"No, not yet, but it's kind of hard to hide something that big. Look, I know that you can't do any jumping or running, but if you want to tag along, in the morning, you can."

"I wouldn't miss it, for the world!"

"We plan to hit the door at 4:30am. Warrants are being prepared right now."

"That works for me!"

CLICK.

It's still hard to believe, that this whole mess started with just one little girl. I've been so caught up in it, that I haven't talked to her or her parents. I hope that Terri doesn't think that I've abandoned her. I also wonder, if she has any idea, of what's going on. Since I've met her, six people have lost their lives, there have been two attempts on my own life, and an innocent family is about to be uprooted, from their home.

None of this is Terri's fault, and if our society had more concern for inner city kids, those people may still be alive. The same mentality has reached suburban kids, as well, and if that's not enough, we now have scum bags, from other countries, contributing!

I almost wish that the captain hadn't called me. I was doing fine before then. I poured myself a shot of Jack and tried to relax. Well, that went over great, because I got another phone call. This time, it was from the last person on Earth, that should be calling me. There was no point, in me using a kind greeting.

"Mr. Councilman, are you out of your freaking mind!"

"Now, that's no way to greet an old friend!"

"Look, honey, if you want to sabotage your own career, then go for it, but leave mine out of it!"

"All that I wanted to do, was invite you to come and hear me speak."

"Speak where? Who the hell, is willing to come within a hundred yards, of you?"

"I'm speaking over in the Pilsen community, at a weekend soccer tournament. It's an attempt at getting more American kids, into the game."

"I didn't know that you were such, a big fan!"

"I'm trying to rekindle my reputation, downtown."

"Once a politician, always a politician!"

"Now, that really hurt, Ricki! Look, honey, I'm just asking you to be a good sport, and support an old friend."

"I'm still in hot water, and I can't make any promises. By the way, thanks for asking about the attempt on my life!"

"Jesus, Ricki, it slipped my mind. I'm sorry!"

"That's OK, I'm fine!"

CLICK.

And politicians wonder why people hate them! I used to think that this man was kind of gutsy, and had balls. It turned me on a little, but now, I think that he's just plain stupid!

32

CREW MEETING

Rafael and his crew had quite a night. For starters, after transferring the girls to the new trailer, his driver did get back on the toll way, but he headed south, not north. In the Pilsen community, Rafael already had a designated spot, to stash the rig. The location, was an old A & P grocery warehouse, that's been abandoned for decades. He chose it, because it had several, old beat-up trailers, parked behind it, and also the remains of the warehouse. The people in the neighborhood were so used to this eye sore, that no one would notice, the new addition.

The girls would be spending another day, in their sheet metal prison, before starting their new lives in America. So far, the entire adventure has done nothing, but strip them of their dignity and hope, just the kind of girls TJ loves to have, in his stable. It's now past midnight and on Saturday morning, they'll be moved to the house, on 61st Street.

TJ, Rafael, and the drivers from down south, were sitting at a bar in the Pilsen area. They were having a pre-victory celebration, when I became the topic of discussion. Rafael had questions, that needed answers.

"TJ, my friend, tell me something. Why is that red head cop, still alive?"

"Man, Rafael, I was wondering the same, damn thing! I'm starting to think that this chick has nine lives!"

"Perhaps, we've been sending boys, to do a man's job, my friend!"

"I'll tell you what, amigo, after we conclude our business on Saturday, I'll finish her off, myself!"

"I'll drink to that! Bartender, more Tequila, all around!"

As they continued partying, I continued trying to get as much sleep, as I could. I set my alarm for 3:00 AM, so that I could make it to my 4:30am appointment. I figured that I'd have plenty of time to get my act together and be present at the raid. It seemed like, I was only asleep for twenty minutes, when I heard the annoying sound of my alarm, going off. I slowly sat up and rubbed my eyes. Doing everything in stages, the second stage was getting up, to make a pot of coffee. I didn't know if I was getting better, or just getting used to the pain, but things were going alright.

By 3:40 AM, I was ready to walk out the door, but that was mostly, because I slept with my clothes on. My final step, was strapping on my vest. Once that I was inside the unmarked squad, I turned on the radio. I was hoping to hear some chatter, but then it dawned on me, that silence would be maintained, regarding this operation. The sun was hanging, just below the horizon, waiting to show her face. I turned off the Ave., onto 61st Street, and cut my headlights. I rolled slowly, and when I got two houses down from TJ's place, I could see the silhouettes of our guys, surrounding the place. I got out of my squad and walked around, to the opposite side of it. I drew my weapon and pointed at the house. Just as I got into position, I could hear the battering ram, knocking the door off of the hinges.

Suddenly, there were lights everywhere and multiple voices yelling, POLICE! I waited a few moments, didn't hear any shots being fired, so I came around the squad and approached the house. Two officers wearing S.W.A.T. gear and carrying automatic weapons, stepped out of the house first, and I quickly flashed my badge. They were followed by Captain Keller. The first thing that I noticed, was the disappointed look on his face.

"Let me guess, He's not, in there, is he?"

"There's no one, but teenage girls, which means that he's more than likely, with that truck and the new recruits."

"Well Captain, I'm sure that this whole damn neighborhood, knows that we're here, and someone's on the horn, right now, telling him that his little love factory, is out of business!"

"You know, Ricki. His Benz is parked in the back. It's a damn shame, that it wasn't named in the warrant! I'd love to take it and see if Lewis and Wilcox, step up to the plate!"

"I don't think that it would be worth, our time. They'll just say, that it was stolen."

Just then, eight girls in handcuffs, were marched out of the house. Seven of them were Latina, and one was African American. It broke my heart, to see it happening.

"Look, Detective, we're going to be here for a while, taking this place apart. Hopefully, we'll find some kind of lead. Why don't you go on, home?"

Instead of going home, I did something that I haven't done in years. I drove to Grant Park. Every now and then, I have the need to be around normal people. It was still early, when I picked my spot on a bench, to do some people watching. At this time of the morning, joggers, are getting their run on. The lake was calm as the city was just beginning to wake up. I was so at peace with myself, that I hadn't noticed that two hours had gone by.

Activity in the park increased, and the day was in full bloom. My expectations had been met, and I felt alive again. Just the medicine that I needed. I kept telling myself, that someday, this will be me. I'd love to live down here, but on a cop's salary, I don't think so!

My cellphone vibrated, and when I reached for it, it shocked me right back, into the real world, because I felt the designer fabric, of my vest. God! What were these people, thinking, when they looked at me? It never dawned on me, to take the stupid thing, off!

"This is Detective Cliff."

"This is the Captain. We've got a knife, with blood stains on it. I'm going to have it dusted for prints and check the bloodstains for DNA. If we're lucky, the prints will belong to TJ, and the blood will belong to Tommy G."

"This case, just keeps getting better and better!"

CLICK.

With my mind in Neverland, I stood up, without paying attention to my surroundings, and stepped right into the path of a bicyclist. The rider tried to stop, but went around me, flipped over, and ended up lying in the grass!

Oh my God, I screamed!

"I'm so sorry! I wasn't paying attention!"

The sudden twist to my body trying to react, was painful as hell, and for some crazy reason, the bicyclist started laughing! The rider then removed their helmet and shades, while still laughing.

Well, I'll be damned! It was Linda, the young officer!"

"What the hell, are you doing, down here?"

"I take a ride through the park, when ever possible, just to keep in shape."

"Really, I can't believe it!"

"Well, actually, I keep thinking, that I'm going to meet a guy, that's not a jerk."

"So, how's that working for you?"

"It's not. They're outnumbered by hot girls, but I keep trying, and in the meantime, I stay in shape."

"Well, I have to hand it to you. You've got a great attitude."

"So, what are you doing here, Ricki?"

"Me? Well, sometimes I feel the need to be around happy people, doing happy things. Dodging bullets, and putting people in jail, is no way to live, not to mention, that lately, I haven't done either, very well!"

"Well Ricki, how would you feel, about a little breakfast?"

"Where are we going to find breakfast, around here?"

"Right over there!"

She pointed at a vendor, pushing a cart, and selling snow cones.

"Come on, it's my treat!"

She walked her bike, and I tagged along. She got an orange flavored snow cone, while I got a rainbow cone. It made me feel like a kid, again.

"Wow, I haven't had one of these, in ages!"

"So, Ricki, when are you going to tell me, what's going on?"

"Well, it's a very long story, and it's tied to a case that I've been working on, for a while now. It involves the trafficking of young girls, from south of the border."

"Let me guess, it's also the reason why there's a contract hit, out on you."

"Look around. Do you see anyone else, wearing a vest?"

"You were right! I don't want to get involved. What's next, on your agenda?"

"Honestly, I don't know."

"Well, take care of yourself. I've got a lot of ground, to cover."

33

TERRI'S SURPRISE

My morning at the lake front, ended up more interesting than I anticipated. Running into Linda was a shock, not to mention, an eye opener. As time goes by, I'm learning that there's more to her, than meets the eye. The truth is, had she been willing to stay, I could've talked to her a lot longer. Sharing the snow cones with her, was a real blast!

It was a little before 11:00 AM and I was just leaving the lake front. The Captain had given me the day off, and I could've used a little nap, but I decided to pay Terri a visit instead.

I took my usual route, through the hospital and stopped at the nurse's station, that I'm known at. For some reason, all of the nurses had big smiles on their faces, but no one let me in, on what was going on. I made my way to Terri's room, and found it empty, except for her belongings. I went back into the hall, and the nurses all, pointed toward the waiting room. I immediately, froze, when I entered the waiting room. I couldn't believe my eyes! Sitting at a round table, was Terri and her parents, talking. This was a milestone, and I didn't know if I should interrupt or not. Terri must've sensed my presence and turned around. She called my name as if, we were old friends.

"Detective Cliff, come over and join us."

I didn't know how to react, but I couldn't pass up the chance. As I held my waist, while sitting down, I got warm hellos from her parents. I was a bit speechless.

"So, it looks like, there's been some new developments, since I've been away."

The three of them, all looked at each other, and finally, Terri spoke up.

"Well, Detective, I thought that you had given up on me. After a few days of loneliness and depression, one of my nurses took matters into her own hands."

"What exactly, did she do?"

"She brought in the hospital chaplain, Father McFarland."

"You're kidding! What did he say, that I hadn't?"

"Actually, he repeated what you had told me, and then he made me see, that I'd already hit rock bottom, and there was no place for me to go, except up. He was very relentless, and since then, he's been counseling the three of us."

In my mind, I was thinking that, I don't get this kid! Perhaps, it was me being naïve and forgetting, that people in her position aren't known for opening up to cops. I treated her like, she was my own daughter and went to wall, trying to make her see the light! I have all of the respect in the world, for the man of cloth, and his mission to save souls, but the lost lambs, the scum bags, and the streets, are my parish, as well as his. Had Terri not been in this hospital, it's not likely, that the chaplain would've crossed her path, but I did. In any case, I'm happy for her, and her parents.

"First of all, I want to say how sorry I am, for making you folks think, that I'd given up on you. So many things have happened, since I last saw you all."

Terri's dad spoke, next.

"The Mrs. and I have been watching the news, and when you were shot outside that liquor store, well, we just thought the worst. It made us take a close look at ourselves and count our blessings. The chaplain helped us, to reevaluate our lives. We reached the conclusion, that the three of us are all that we have, and had we continued the way that we were, each of us would've lost a great deal. I guess that what I'm trying to say is, that as a family, we owe you so much!"

"Seeing the three of you talking, and working as a unit, means the world to me. So, Miss Terri, what's the next step, in your new life?"

"As soon as I get out of here, my dad has hired a tutor, to help me study for my G.E.D."

"That's great news!"

"After that, we're going on a family vacation, to get reacquainted."

"That sounds wonderful! Well folks, I hate to go, but it's time for me to leave. You guys keep in touch, and I'll always make time for you."

I left the hospital, floating on cloud nine! Times like these, make my whole stinking job, worth it all. I can't wait to tell the Captain, the good news.

When I got home, I was pretty beat and it wasn't just because of my early morning appointment, but also, the fact that I hadn't given my ribs the rest, that they need. After getting partially, undressed, my next move was to remove my bandages. They had loosened up, and were beginning to get rather funky, I might add! Using a pair of scissors, I carefully cut and removed them. The fresh air against my skin, felt so incredibly good, that I decided to go without for a while. Hopefully, later on, I can get Linda to re-wrap some fresh ones.

Just as I was about to close my eyes, my phone rang. I didn't recognize the number, but answered. To my surprise, it turned out to be the Motor Pool, at work. You've got to love these guys, because they don't beat around the bush! They made it very clear, that my bike, which isn't an official vehicle, was taking up valuable space in their garage. In other words, come and get your crap! Great, just what I needed! I don't even know any motorcycle cops, that could help me out, and even if I did, I don't think that it would matter. My only choice now, is to rent a trailer, and maybe the good people at the pool, will be willing to help me, mount the damn thing on it.

Since I was awake, I decided to call the captain, and give him the good news, about Terri.

"Good afternoon, Captain."

I could tell, right away, that he was burned out.

"We still haven't found Rafael, or the girls, if that's what you want, but I did get a message from the Motor Pool!"

"Why the hell, did they call you? I already talked to those guys!"

"Well, just do something, about it! I don't need this crap!"

"I already have plans, Captain, and by the way, I saw Terri and her parents."

"How is she, doing?"

"You're not going to, believe this, but she's doing great! She and her parents are being counseled by the hospital chaplain, and they've made a complete turnaround! She'll be going home soon and has quite a future. Do you know what, this means, Captain? It means that we finally, won one!"

"Well, at least something good, has come from this mess! I'm glad to hear it. Look, I've to go."

"OK, Captain."

CLICK.

It felt great, to give the Captain the good news, even though he sounded like, he should be lying down, too. I got comfortable again, and not two minutes later, my phone rang, and it was the Captain again.

"I thought that you may want to know, that I just got a call from the Chief. He wants to pull D.M.V. photos of TJ and Rafael and go public with the media."

"That should ruffle their feathers! I get the feeling that once that they see their faces on the air, they're going to make a move, either tonight or first thing in the morning."

"The Chief also wants to put a full court press, on every punk on the street, so that they'll be out of our way."

"Why not, shake down Sally's?"

"I doubt that they'll be there, but that's a good idea."

"You know, Captain. This is going to be like turning the light on cock roaches!"

34

PANIC MODE

etween the Chicago P.D. and the Illinois State Troopers, everyone in law enforcement, was getting tired of this whole mess. To make matters worse, the city is preparing an all-out, five-star funeral service, including bagpipes, for our fallen comrades, the two crooked vice squad cops. What a load of crap!

What really sucks is, that usually, in a case like this, we'd have the Mayor, the Chief of Police, and several other dignitaries, speaking at the service. Tears will be shed by the families left behind, sympathy will be felt across the city, and the media will milk it, for all it's worth. The citizens will never know that they were once partners in crime, with the very same men, that took their lives.

I finally, got around to asking Linda to redo my bandages. There was no way that I could've done it myself. It was going to be painful, either way, but it at least she'd do a good job. When I spoke to her, she said that she'd been wondering, when I was going to get around to it. She had a briefing to go to, before her shift started, and would have time following it, so we agreed to meet at the exercise room. A couple of hours later, I found her standing, outside of the entrance.

"Thanks for doing this, Linda."

"No problem, how's it going?"

"I've had better days!"

"Are you still in a lot of pain?"

"Yeah, but this time, it's a pain in my ass! It's about my bike. The Motor

Pool has been leaving messages, all over the damn place! It's not an official vehicle, and they want it out of their way."

"Well, I'm pressed for time right now, so let's get these bandages on, and maybe we can fix that problem later."

"You're kidding me, right?"

"Remember that I told you that I grew up, with all brothers? When we were kids, we rode motor cross."

"My God, you're just full of surprises! Next, you're going to tell me, that you ride bulls, too! You don't, do you?"

"Come on Ricki, let's get this over with."

I don't know if it was because she was in a hurry or not, but man, did she wrap the bandages tight! With all the help that she was giving me, I was afraid to say anything. I have to admit that the added support, really did help, but it was a reminder of what I'd been through.

The wheels of justice were turning quickly, and halfway through the evening, the faces of Rafael and TJ were being plastered on every network in the Midwest, and nationwide on CNN, Fox, and CSPAN. There was no place, these guys could go, without being recognized.

Once that the good folks out at Lewis and Wilcox, heard the news, they went straight into panic mode and started blowing up Rafael's phone, with messages. He totally ignored them, because at the time, he had far bigger problems, than dealing with someone that reaps the benefits, but won't get their hands dirty. The fact that he'd become the most wanted man, in America, wasn't going over well, with the cartel, back at home. As of right now, law enforcement has a major fire, growing under his ass, and failure is unacceptable to his superiors.

His mind was frantically racing, and he recalled the first time that he saw me, at Sally's bar. When thinking about it, he got pissed off all over again, regarding the three losers on Harleys, who failed to kill me. From his perspective, he wouldn't be in this mess, if not for me. Due to the trade that he's in, he obviously, doesn't have respect for women, least of all, women who are cops. If he had the time, he'd take me out, himself.

Out south, in Orland Park, Wilcox had just thrown an overnight bag into the back seat, of his car. Not being the smartest one, of the Petreas brothers, he'd planned to bug-out, while the getting was good. The flaw in his plan, was running across the southern border. Without communication with Rafael, he had no idea, that the cartel was pissed off with the Chicago chapter, and he'd be walking right into a hornet's nest.

He stopped at the bank and withdrew as much money as he could, without drawing unwanted attention. He then said goodbye to his lavish life and got on the I-80, headed for Indiana. In about thirty minutes he'll be crossing the Illinois State border, into the state of Indiana. His destination, is Indianapolis International Airport.

So far, neither the law firm, nor his name, had been mentioned on the air, but he didn't want to take the risk, of flying out of O'Hare Airport, in Chicago. He had a three-hour drive, ahead of him, and he knew that he'd have to purchase a round-trip ticket, to Mexico, in order to look normal. He felt bad, for running out on his partner, Cynthia Lewis, at the firm, but he was looking out, for his own ass.

Across the city, word was being spread around the heavier, crime-ridden communities, that something was going down. From the south side, to the west side, to the north side, police informants were being squeezed, for all that they knew. Either people didn't know anything, or they were afraid of Rafael Petreas.

Sally's bar had been flipped over, and it netted a couple of ounces of pot, some crack cocaine, nine handguns, two stolen Harleys, seven bikers who had broken probation, and two bikers that had warrants out, for their arrest. Out of all the people in the bar, not one of them, had ever heard of TJ or Rafael.

Surprise!

Since no one had ever heard of them, they didn't stand in the way, when everything that wasn't nailed down, was confiscated, from the upstairs office.

Without a doubt, it had been a very long day and night, for law enforcement, and tomorrow will prove to be the same. Knowing that tomorrow will be tough, I decided to treat myself to a cocktail. It was a beautiful night for a drive, and I really missed my bike. I can't wait for my ribs, to get a little bit stronger.

I pulled into the parking lot of my new favorite watering hole, and noticed an unmarked, Ford Vicki. I'm guessing that Detective Maxwell Little is inside. When I walked in, I saw him sitting at the bar, talking to that cute Asian bartender. I climbed up on the stool next to him, with a grimace on my face, from the pain.

Well, it sure is good to see you, said Max.

"You know, most people don't greet me, this way!"

The bartender had remembered me and sat a shot of Jack and a beer, in front of me.

"Yeah, well, most people don't have a captain, that's flipping out! I know that it has something to do with TJ and this Rafael guy, but there has to be more."

"With all that you've done for me, you deserve the whole scoop, Max. TJ and Rafael are tied to a Mexican Cartel, and they're responsible for the trooper that was murdered, out on the interstate. He was killed, because they were hauling a load of teenage girls, from south of the border. These girls are used as stock, for TJ's stable. By the way, the two Vice Squad cops, that the city is planning the big service for, well, they were the cartels inside connection, until I set them up, and Rafael killed them, at that truck stop, in Elmhurst."

"So, where is the truck load of girls, at?"

"That's the million-dollar question!"

"Let me take, a guess? You were a bit, too nosy, and that's why they tried to kill you, twice."

"Bingo! You've got it, buddy! There's also a Gucci law firm, out in Orland Park, that's involved."

"Don't tell me, that's who's been bouncing TJ, all of these years!"

"Well, they did have a little help, from the Feds! So far, we've got bodies piling up at the morgue, and I'm expecting more."

35

CHANGE OF PLANS

While Max and I were relaxing and enjoying a cold one, the scene was quite the opposite, with Rafael and his crew. The five of them were holding up at a motel, in the Pilsen area, and he had already kicked the TV screen in, after seeing his face broadcasted, one too many times. Their entire plan was screwed up, and as of right now, it was quickly becoming, a game of survival.

Rafael and TJ, had already held a secret meeting, and had agreed, that this was the end of their run, together. Over the years, they'd made a lot of money and lived a good life. Even though their comrades from Texas, had been loyal, they decided to throw them, under the bus. They needed to buy some time, by creating a diversion. TJ knew that we had tossed his house, but still, they instructed the Texas boys, to dump the girls off there. To make it look good, Rafael paid them off, for their services.

He also told them, to get lost and don't attempt to cross the border, for a while. Because of their ties to the cartel, he knew that even if they got busted, by the cops, they wouldn't talk. He informed them that a maxi-length van would be parked between two trailers, at the abandoned warehouse. Their instructions were to transfer the girls to the van, drop them off at TJ's place, and get the hell out of town.

TJ and Rafael had planned to take off, during the wee hours of the morning. As for Rafael, his plan was to hold up in the southeast section of the city, in a Hispanic community, until he comes up with a better plan. TJ, was headed to the hood, where there were plenty of brothers, who would do favors for him.

Once that their meeting was completed, a bottle of Tequila was opened, and the drinking began. After the hours passed, a second bottle was opened. It wasn't long before Rafael, got a bright idea.

"TJ, my friend, how do you feel about one more mission, for old time's sake?"

"What do you have, in mind?"

"Why don't we pay our friend, the red-haired senorita, a little visit, and have a fiesta with her, and then, cut her throat!"

"Rafael, my friend, I can't think of a better way, to say goodbye to her! Salute."

They toasted and shared a creepy, disgusting, laugh.

The effects of the alcohol caused them all, to oversleep. One of the Texas boys was first, to awake up, and he alerted the others. Pressed for time, now, Rafael gave the boys a hug and sent them, on their way.

During the wee hours of the morning, Wilcox touched down in Mexico City. So far, he had escaped the madness in Chicago, and hopefully, it would only be a matter of time, before he heard from his brother. He arranged to be picked up, and waited for his ride. He knew that soon, Lewis would be trying to contact him, but he'd have to ignore her. As far as he was concerned, that part of his life was gone, forever.

At the abandoned warehouse, the Texas boys, who drove the pick-up, arrived. As for the driver of the big rig, his job was done. He'd only stayed around to party and get paid. As of right now, he's in the wind. After opening the big doors on the back of the trailer, one of them stood clear with a pistol in his hand, while the other, made the girls climb out. They had been in darkness for so long, that they had problems, adjusting to the sunlight, and that made it easier, to force them into the maxi-van. Once that they were all loaded into the van, they took off, and that's when the chaos started.

There was uncontrollable crying and screaming! The guy riding shotgun, turned around and waved his pistol, at the girls, forcing them to quiet down and behave. They were now in route to the south side, in search of TJ's place.

178

The Texas boys, were in a strange city, and their nerves were starting to get the best of them. Every time that someone looked their way, it freaked them out. In addition to that, they had no idea of what they were going to do, after delivering the girls. The city was slowly waking up, and traffic was getting heavy. They began to get a little relaxed, because most of the people, walking down the street, were Hispanic.

As they drove through town, they got more and more comfortable. They had no idea that Rafael was hanging them out to dry, and TJ's place, would be crawling with cops.

36

TOTAL CHAOS

I t was just past 8:30am, and Councilman Lee was enjoying an early breakfast, in a cafeteria at Daley Center, downtown. After eating, he had time to go over the speech he'd prepared, for later this morning. He wore a warm-up suit, to show that he's sports minded. Being honest with himself, he knew that most of the people in the Pilsen community, had never heard of him. Being optimistic, he also believed, that the very same fact, may work in his favor. This is an opportunity to build new relationships, without being judged by his past. He looked at his watch, because it was time for his Town Car, to pick him up.

The ride across town, gave him time to go online and educate himself on some of the hot, current, soccer topics. It wouldn't hurt to look like, he actually knows something, about the sport.

On my end, I had no reason, to get up at the crack of dawn, so I started my morning in a leisurely fashion. At the same time, I was keeping an open mind, in case I had to leave in a hurry, due to a break in the case. I started a pot of coffee and turned on the tube, while it was brewing. In the bathroom, I took the closest thing to a shower, that I could, without getting my bandages wet and messy. After carefully, putting on a pair of jeans, I stuck my feet into my slippers and headed for the coffee pot.

As I sat down on the sofa, I noticed that the TV was showing a scene, of what looked like, the desert. In the background, were four green and white, Border Patrol vehicles, with officers standing around. The camera then panned over to what appeared to be a body, under a plastic tarp. The camera continued to pan over, about 5 or 6 feet, to a smaller plastic tarp, that had something round, under it. Based on what's been going on along the border, these days, I assumed, that what I was watching, was the result of the ongoing war, between different cartels. This kind of thing is so commonplace, now, that I wasn't that much, into the report, but then something happened, that got my full attention. A window appeared in the upper left-hand corner of the screen, and it showed a passport picture, of David Wilcox.

That's when I grabbed the remote and turned up the volume, on my set. I caught the tail end of the reporter, saying, that he was identified by articles found on him, but the official identification, will be made through examination, by the coroner.

I'm thinking that Wilcox saw the broadcast of Rafael, and got nervous. Evidently, he ran back across the border, seeking a haven with the cartel, but they weren't feeling it! If that's true, they must be aware that the Chicago chapter, is in deep shit, and Rafael is next! This may be a good time, to tighten up the screws, on Miss Lewis, out at the firm. I'd better give the captain, a call.

In a very tired voice, he answered.

"Captain, it's me Ricki. I just saw a live report, from the desert, along the Mexican border. You're not going to believe this, but it looks like, the cartel has beheaded Wilcox."

"Are you talking about, David Wilcox?"

"Yes sir! They showed a passport photo of him, on the screen. Captain, you know what this means, don't you?"

"Yeah, they caught one of our Broadcast, and they'll be going after Rafael, next. Breaking up this trafficking ring has taken a big bite, out of their pocketbook! Evidently, it's not going over very big, back home."

"You know Captain, I was thinking that maybe, we can send someone out south, to put the squeeze on Miss Lewis."

"Well, so far, she hasn't done anything, except provide representation, but the D.A. may be interested in serving her with a subpoena, later. I'll tell you what, why don't we hold off for now, and keep a pair of eyes, on her movements?"

"OK Captain, keep in touch."

CLICK.

37

MAYHEM ON THE STREETS

Councilman Lee was wearing out the keys, on his laptop, as he rode across town, in the back of his Town Car. There was more information available on soccer, than he had time for. He scrolled through a lot of it, just looking at teams, superstar players, and things of that nature. He could see why there was such a push, to get American kids more involved, in it. He realized that the market around the world, was huge, and he made a mental note to do further research later, to see what American investors were into this. For now, he was more concerned with the highlights, that may be beneficial to the speech, that he'll be giving.

For starters, he learned that teams, like Real Madrid and Barcelona, were among the forerunners of the sport, but the teams to beat, who captivated the audience, were Brazil and Argentina. Among the superstars of the game, were players like Messi and Ronaldo. On a small piece of paper, he wrote down all that he had learned. His task was to incorporate it into today's speech, without using his notes.

Just minutes away, our Texas boys were in traffic, and trying to keep the girls under control. Emotions were on high, and they were getting more frantic, as the van moved along. Some of the girls were uncontrollably crying, while others were freaked out, by the unknown environment, surrounding them.

They were headed southbound on Ashland Ave., when they passed a blue and white squad car, headed north bound. Three of the girls saw the squad and started banging on the windows, while screaming! The cop that was driving, saw them. He couldn't make out what they were saying, but he knew that they were frightened. Immediately, he hit his lights and siren. Interrupting traffic, he made a U-turn, in pursuit of the van, as his partner got on the radio, requesting back-up.

The driver of the van had already started panicking, when he saw the squad go by them, and when he saw it turn around in his mirror, he floored the gas pedal. As they were weaving through traffic, our two boys started arguing in Spanish, as the girls got more hysterical! They increased their speed as the cops got closer to them. The driver was beginning to watch his mirror more than the traffic, in front of him. He blew through a couple of stop signs, barely avoiding other vehicles.

Councilman Lee's Town Car was west bound on 18th Street, just a few blocks from Harrison Park, the site for the soccer tournament.

Up ahead, the van driver saw a traffic signal and decided to go for it, no matter what. At one hundred feet away, the signal had already turned yellow, but he floored the gas pedal, anyway. When he reached the intersection, a black Town Car was passing through, right in front of him. He hit the Town Car right behind the back door, spinning it around and sending it across the double yellow lines, head-on, into oncoming traffic. His decision to do this, caused a major pile-up, with four other vehicles.

In the meantime, the van kept on going with steam, coming from the radiator, a cracked windshield, all, while dragging the front bumper and leaving a trail of motor oil. Behind them now, were three squad cars in hot pursuit! At the next intersection, was Harrison Park, where two squads had set-up, a roadblock, sitting bumper to bumper. Standing outside the squads, were two officers with shotguns. At this point, the driver of the van decided to go down, with his boots on.

In his mirror, the driver saw paramedics, fire engines, and more cops, than he's ever seen in his life! He knew that they'd never let them live, and he was on a mission, to take as many of them with him, as he could! He crossed his chest and headed straight for the roadblock, at full speed. At the last second, the two cops jumped out of the way, just before the van smashed into the squad cars, separating them. The van went right between them, but lost control, when it hit the curb. That caused the van to flip over, before landing on the roof and sliding into a row of parked minivans and SUVs.

Both front doors of the van popped open. The driver jumped out and ran into the crowd of soccer players and their families. Our other Texas boy, climbed out with his gun drawn, which was a big mistake! By that time, the two cops on foot, had caught up to them. One cop put a round of shotgun pellets into his chest, and the other one put a round in the side of his head! They then, ran into the park, in pursuit of the driver.

The girls had been tossed around like socks, in a dryer! Some of them were knocked out cold, some had multiple fractures, and some had broken glass, embedded in their skin. By now, the air was swarming with helicopters. Two were law enforcement, but the rest were all media, from local news networks. The park and the surrounding area, was a complete, disaster!

38

HOLY MOLY!

I was still at home, when I saw the coverage, of what was happening at Harrison Park. There was so much going on, that even with all the coverage, I was still missing bits and pieces. At one accident scene, a black Town Car was involved. The driver had been pronounced dead, at the scene, and identified as a chauffeur, working for a local limo service. The passenger's name was withheld and rushed to an area hospital's trauma unit. I started putting pieces together, and realized that this was the day, that Councilman Lee was scheduled to speak at a soccer tournament, in the same area.

I immediately, took out my phone and tried to reach him. All that I got was his voice mail. I waited fifteen minutes, tried it again, and got the same result. I was sure that it was him. I called the captain, but he didn't answer, either. As soon as I hung up, my phone rang in my hand.

"It's me, the Captain! I think that we have a lead, on the girls! Get over to Harrison Park, in the Pilsen area!"

"Wait a minute! You mean that they're caught up in that circus, over there?"

"They could be. A van, carrying young Hispanic girls, was involved in a high-speed chase, that ended in a shooting. The driver is still on the run."

"Captain, a black Town Car was involved also, and I think that Councilman Lee was inside of it!"

"Jesus Christ, what's next?"

"See you there, Cap!"

CLICK.

While I was talking to the Captain, the entire park, was being surrounded by law enforcement. At one entrance to the park, police were escorting families out, and sending them away from the chaos, hoping that it would make it easier, to spot the driver of the van.

The driver, himself, was now running for his life! In addition to the cops, scattering, all over the place, he now had an angry mob, of pissed off fathers, who had ignored the cops, trying to get their hands on him. Apparently, during his attempt to escape, he knocked down, and trampled several women and their children. As he crisscrossed through the park, dodging obstacles, he would periodically, look over his shoulder, to see how close the mob was. On one such occasion, he failed to see a folded down, baby stroller, that had been left behind, when all the madness started.

He tripped over it, going down, face first, and tried to throw his body into a roll, but never had a chance, to get back on his feet. He was like a fly, caught in spider's web, as the angry mob pounced on him. There were so many of them, over him, and around him, that he couldn't see daylight! With all, that he'd done, in the last few days, I'd doubt, that he had any idea, that he'd end up, being the victim of street justice.

When the cops arrived, at the scene, the mob scattered, and they made no attempt, to try and catch any of them. He had been beaten, nearly to death. His face was unrecognizable, as a human being, he barely had a pause, and was fading quickly. As the cops waited for the arrival of the EMT's, they watched him, take his last breath.

Back at my place, I put on my vest, packed my gear, and I was ready, to go. I reached for the door knob and turned it. That's when the door flew open, and for a split second, I thought, that I saw a big fist, coming right at me. Everything went black, and I was out COLD!!

While I was unconscious, the Pilsen area had been all, but shut down. Harrison Park, had become a media circus. Tow trucks were in action, and the media was interviewing anyone, willing to go on the air, live. The police, were taking statements, from dozens of people, who had witnessed events, from the accident scene, as well as, the shooting at the squad car road block, and the beat down, of the van driver. The hand gun used by one of the Texas boys, in the van, was recovered at the scene. We would later find out, that it was also used, to kill Illinois State Trooper, Roy Clemens.

The Captain had been making his rounds and getting reports, from uniform officers that responded to the original call, for back-up. During that time, he would periodically, look at his watch. He was beginning to wonder why, I hadn't arrived at the park, yet. He called the station house and talked to the desk sergeant, to see if I'd showed up, for some reason. Being told no, only made him pissed off. With all that had happened, there was still the matter of tracking down, TJ and Rafael. The Captain had no choice, but to focus on the task at hand. Unfortunately, I had a history of going off, on some wild tangent, and he'd made up his mind, to deal with me later.

Feeling like, I was coming out of a bad dream, my head was throbbing, and when I tried to reach for my temple, I couldn't. That's when I realized, that my hands, as well as both my ankles, were tied to the post of my bed. I had been stripped down, to my bra and panties, and then it dawned on me, that loud music was filling the air.

I had no idea of what had happened to me, or who was behind it. The only thing that I knew for sure, was, that I was helpless! My purse had been thrown on the floor, and the top edge of my phone was exposed. I could see the red-light flashing, indicating that I had messages. It was a small relief, to know that someone was looking for me. My mind told me, that it had to be, the captain. I wanted to believe that he'd come here, if for no other reason, than to chew me out, but with all that was happening, he's got a ton on his plate, already.

My thoughts were rudely interrupted, when my worst nightmare, walked into my bedroom. I struggled to break free, when I saw standing before me, were Rafael and TJ. Both, with shit eating grins on their faces! TJ stood with my bottle of Jack Daniels in his hand, as Rafael, approached the side of my bed.

"It's nice of you to join us, senorita!"

He was so close to me, that I could smell the bourbon, on his breath.

191

That's when I spit in his face, and he took advantage of the bandages around my mid-section, by punching me in the ribs. If it wasn't for the loud music, I'm sure that my neighbors, would have heard me scream! As I laid there enduring the pain, TJ stepped over to my other side.

"So, you're the bitch, that screwed up our little game! If it wasn't for you, Tommy G. would still be around, but you couldn't mind, your own damn business. Tell me something, Detective. How is that little whore, Terri, doing?"

At this point, I had nothing to lose.

"Fuck you, Thaddeus!"

"Now, that kind of attitude, is only going to make your death, be slow and painful."

"What's the matter, Thaddeus? You're only man enough, to handle little girls?"

I felt the end coming and didn't think that it would matter, rather I talked shit to him, or not. Of course, he didn't care for my comment, and with the speed of lightning, he whipped out a knife, cut my bra strap, exposing my boobs, and leaving a trail of blood. Not showing fear, was all, that I had left. At least I'd die, knowing that their human trafficking game, had been dismantled.

39

CANDEE'S DUMB MOVE

Councilman Lee, was recovering from surgery, in a private hospital room. He had sustained two broken ribs, a bruised lung, a fractured left fibula, and due to a concussion, he was experiencing poor vision and hearing lose, in one ear. The doctors said, that under the circumstances, he was lucky. Needless to say, he won't be playing footsie, on his craft, with me, or anyone else, for a long time.

Outside of his room, lurking in the hallway, is the infamous reporter, Candee Harris. She was snooping around, trying to get in, to interview him. He had been given a heavy sedative and was in and out, of consciousness. In addition to that, he was repeatedly, calling out my name, in his sleep. At the nurse's station, at the end of the hallway, two nurses were gossiping about the previous story, that had made the news about our relationship.

Candee, being herself, pretended to be on her cellphone as she slowly walked pass the nurses, eavesdropping, on their conversation. She overheard them saying that the councilman, was repeatedly, calling out my name, in his sleep. With that, she took the ball and ran with it! Minutes later, she was in her little red Porsche, racing to meet her camera crew, at my place. Her plan was to resurrect, the original story. This time, she would start her report with the comment,

LAME DUCK POLITICAL LOVE AFFAIR HAS TRAGIC ENDING!

It was Saturday and Linda had the day off. She thought that she'd do me a favor, by picking up my bike and riding it home, for me.

She walked into the Motor Pool, wearing form-fitting jeans and boots, with her badge clipped to her belt. Being young and attractive, she turned the heads of all the mechanics, on duty. They hadn't noticed her badge, and didn't know that they were barking up, the wrong tree! She mentioned that she was there, on my behalf, and that cast a sour note, throughout the place. Being the pigs that they are, they assumed that we were an item. Thanks to me, this young woman's reputation, was now, tainted.

The Pool supervisor was more than happy, to get my bike out of his hair. Linda decided to give me a call and let me know, that she was on her way, with it. So far, the abuse that I'd been taking, was only verbal, with a slap here and there, leaving me with a bloody, busted lip. Rafael was now drunk, and seemed amused by my boobs, but he wasn't the first man, to touch them. I had been through worse and managed to survive, without being raped. On the floor, I could see the little red light on my phone, blinking again. Thank God, that I had it set on vibrate.

Linda was persistent. She left the Motor Pool and went upstairs to my desk. After not finding me there, she went straight to the captain's office. His door was closed, so she knocked and the captain told her to come in.

"Hi, Captain."

"What are you doing here, Officer?"

"Well sir, I've been trying to locate Detective Cliff, but she hasn't been answering her phone."

"Dammit, that's it!"

"Is something wrong, sir?"

Before he could answer her, his phone rang, and it was the desk sergeant.

"Sorry, to bother you, Captain, but I just got a domestic compliant, from a woman saying that there's unusual loud music, coming from her neighbor's apartment."

"Sergeant, what's the matter with you? You know better than to bother me, with petty stuff!"

"Sir, the complaint is registered at Detective Cliff's place!"

"Holy shit, she's been missing all day! Get a squad over there, right away! Damn it, I forgot about the contract!"

Linda heard him say contract, and my name, and she took off, right away! That's when the captain, went bananas!

"Officer, get back here! Did you hear me? Get back here! That's an order!"

Linda totally ignored the Captain, as she headed for my bike. He was thinking, that I'd did, just what, he was afraid of. I had turned her into another cowboy, just what he needed! Thanks to my nosy neighbor, the Calvary was on the way. It appeared to be a little too late, because Candee Harris, was now at my lobby door, about to do a live report.

HI, I'M CANDEE HARRIS, WITH THE W.L.O.K. NEWS CREW, AND WE'RE COMING TO YOU LIVE FROM OUTSIDE OF THE HOME OF DETECTIVE RICKI CLIFF, OF THE CHICAGO POLICE DEPARTMENT. AS YOU MAY RECALL, SHE WAS PREVIOUSLY NOTED FOR HAVING AN ALLEGED AFFAIR, WITH THE CITY'S OWN, COUNCILMAN LEE. BUT THIS MORNING, THAT AFFAIR TOOK A TRAGIC TURN, WHEN HIS TOWN CAR WAS INVOLVED IN A HORRIBLE ACCIDENT, IN THE PILSEN COMMUNITY. SOURCES TELL US, THAT HE'S BEEN REQUESTING HER FROM HIS HOSPITAL BED, AND WE'RE HERE TO SEE IF THERE'S STILL A SPARK LEFT, TO REKINDLE THAT ROMANCE.

Candee pressed the button next to my name and waited. With the music turned up, to drown out my screams, you could barely hear the doorbell ring, in my apartment. Rafael went to the door and pressed the access button, instead of the intercom. He waited at the door and called out to TJ.

"It looks like we've got company, my friend!"

After waiting a few minutes, he quickly opened the door. By now, Candee, was standing there. He grabbed her by the collar, snatched her into my apartment, and threw her on the sofa, like she was a rag doll. TJ then broke out, into laughter.

"It's party time now, baby!"

My neighbor, across the hall, had been watching the whole thing, through her peep hole, and that's when she started blowing up the desk sergeant's phone again! He got on the radio and contacted the Captain, who was already in route to my place.

"Captain, I just got another call from that neighbor. She says that a large Hispanic man just opened Ricki's door, and snatched a female visitor, inside!"

"Damn it, Sergeant, that's Rafael! Get that damn place surrounded!"

"Sir, there's more! That reporter, Candee Harris, was doing a live report, from outside Ricki's place, and now she's missing!"

"Jesus Christ, that's just what I freaking needed! He's got her nosy ass, too!"

Linda had pulled up, on my bike, and with my welfare on her mind, she didn't notice the news van, across the street. They had the cameras rolling when she parked, and removed her back-up weapon from her boot. It was all being broadcast live, on W.L.O.K. She chose a doorbell other than mine, and when she got an answer, she identified herself as a Chicago Police Officer. She was buzzed in, and began evacuating all the residents of the building. Those people were lucky, because it was a move, that I never would've thought of.

40

IT'S NOW OR NEVER

The Captain was next, to show up to the party. When he pulled up, he saw my bike and about thirty people, standing in front of my building. He identified himself, then started questioning people. They told him that they had been evacuated by a female officer, who was now in the building. He moved the group down, to the end of the block. Despite Linda, already being inside, he had to go by the book. He hated the fact, that the news vans were across the street, watching his every move, but there was nothing, that he could do about it, as long as they kept their distance.

Linda made her way to my neighbor's apartment, and was watching my place, through the peep hole. She was hoping that she'd be hearing sirens and helicopters overhead, by now, but she wasn't. She began losing her patience, and was getting nervous.

In my apartment, Candee had been stripped down to her panties and bra, and tied up, as well. This time, being nosy, had gotten her a front seat in Hell, and she was terrified!

Across the hall, Linda thought it was now or never, so she made her move. She stepped out, banged on my door, and ran back inside my neighbor's apartment. The door quickly opened, and TJ stepped out, with a gun in his hand. He looked in both directions, not seeing anyone. He walked down the hallway toward the elevator, with his back turned. That's when Linda stepped back out and yelled POLICE! TJ quickly turned around and she put three rounds, from her pistol, into his chest!

He never had a chance! She then, ran back inside the apartment and was leaning against the door, breathing heavily! She had never been in this position before and didn't know what, to do next. The music was so loud in my place, that we didn't hear the shots, being fired.

Rafael, was beginning to have fun with Candee, which took some of the pressure off me. I was still tied up, but I was wondering, what I could do with this opportunity, that's been given to me. It wasn't long, before Rafael started wondering, what was taking TJ so long. Well, at least he had a strange expression, on his face. He looked out into the hallway and saw TJ dead, lying in a pool of his own blood. He came back in and went straight to the window. That's when he saw that the building was surrounded by S.W.A.T., and behind them, was a total media circus. He knew that there was only one way out, and he was determined, to go down with his boots on!

A marksman, with a scope on his rifle, saw him in the window and notified the Captain. The Captain, then got on the P.A.

"Attention, Rafael Petreas and Thaddeus James, this is Captain Keller, with the Chicago Police Department. We have the building surrounded. Drop your weapons and come out, with your hands up."

Linda felt relieved. She had been dying to hear from back-up and now she was able to think, like a well-trained officer, again. Even though the madness wasn't over yet, I too, was beginning to feel better. Rafael, was wearing out the carpet, in my place. Fifteen minutes had passed since he'd heard from the Captain, and he was pacing back and forth. He picked up the bottle of Jack, drank the remainder, and in a moment of rage, threw the bottle out the window, getting the captain's attention.

The Captain called out his name, over the P.A.

"Rafael, there's no way out! It doesn't have to end, this way. All of the members of your crew are gone, and we have the girls. It's just you and TJ! You guys are alone, now! Give it up! We'll give you ten more minutes, and then we're coming in!"

At this point, S.W.A.T. was already in place throughout the building, and was waiting for the command, to storm my apartment. Rafael went into a panic, grabbed Candee, and took her to the window, with his gun to her head, and in his strong, Mexican accent, he yelled out.

"I'm warning you cops, if you don't back off, I'm going to start, killing these bitches!

Linda could hear him and she knew that he was preoccupied, so she eased the door open, and tossed her badge down the hall to S.W.A.T., before crawling out of the apartment, on her hands and knees. She made her way out of the building, and over to Captain Keller. As you can imagine, that's when he went berserk!

"That was a dumb-ass move, that you made, Officer! You could've been killed up there, and the next time that I tell you to stop, you'd better freeze, or I swear to God, I'll have your badge!"

"But Captain!"

"Don't give me that, but shit! You've been hanging around that crazy ass Ricki, too much! Now, tell me what the situation is, up there!"

"Well, sir, TJ is gone. I put three rounds into his chest."

"Well, I'll be damned! You're one lucky, young lady! Don't think for one damn minute, that you know what the hell, you're doing! I swear, if Ricki lives, I'm going to strangle her ass!"

"But sir, it's not her fault!"

"I don't want to hear that, but shit! Now, take a walk!"

The Chief of Police, not only had radio contact, but he was fed up, with it all. He contacted the Captain and told him to go in immediately, but the Captain reasoned with him.

"Let me try, one more thing? If it doesn't work, I'm going in."

The light on my phone began to blink, and this time I knew, that it wasn't for me.

Rafael, I yelled!

"What is it, bitch? I'm busy!"

"Look down, at the floor. Do you see my cellphone, ringing? Answer it."

He reached down and picked it up.

"Yeah, who the fuck, is this?"

"It's me, Captain Keller."

"I don't have time, for games, Captain!"

"I don't have time, for games either, Rafael. I just thought that you might want to know, that your brother, is dead."

"You're bullshitting me, Captain! I told you, that I don't have time, for games!"

"It was the Cartel! They beheaded him, and left him in the desert. I'm telling you, the truth."

"You're lying, they wouldn't do that!"

"I have your lawyer, Miss Lewis, on the line. She can tell you."

"Rafael, it's me, and he's not lying! He ran out on us, and went home, but they killed him, and left him in the desert! It's been all over the news!"

The Captain, spoke again.

"Rafael, it's the Captain again. They're going to kill you next! If you want to live, come with me! This is your last chance!"

Rafael hung up the phone and threw it against the wall. At the same time, a flash bang canister, came crashing through the window and my apartment was stormed, by several members of S.W.A.T. Rafael saw three red laser beams, focused on his heart, as we all started gagging and coughing. I screamed at him to give up, and he dropped his weapon. Two S.W.A.T. officers, immediately took him down and handcuffed him. Another one got on his radio and yelled, STAND DOWN! STAND DOWN, THE SUSPECT IS IN CUSTODY!

Two bath robes were taken from my closet, and wrapped around Candee and me, before we were escorted out, behind Rafael. The S.W.A.T. officers and Rafael stepped out, ahead of us. As soon as they cleared the lobby door, a gunshot rang out, and we were pushed down to the ground. I looked up and saw Rafael, lying on the sidewalk, handcuffed. A bullet had gone straight into his forehead, and the Captain immediately, yelled out over his radio.

"Who the hell, fired that shot?"

The S.W.A.T. Commander said, that it wasn't any of his guys. It was then that the Captain realized, that the Cartel had been present, all along, and was just waiting for an opportunity. The S.W.A.T. Commander had his men comb the entire area, searching for the gunman.

Candee and I were taken to the hospital, for a routine examination. However, she was going to need psychological help, as well. As much as she's been a pain in the ass, in the past, I felt sorry for her. Welcome to the real world, honey!

The park, across the street from my place, is lined on one side by a roll of apartment buildings. On the roof of one of those buildings, S.W.A.T. found the gunman's rifle, but he was long gone. Even though the madness was over, there was a ton of clean-up work, and reports to be made, and I'll be at my desk for a long time, buried in that paperwork.

EPILOGUE

The two drivers from Texas were cremated, with the expenses paid by taxpayers. It felt like, it was more than they deserved. All current cases, being handled by the Lewis and Wilcox law firm, were instead being temporarily represented, by Cook County's Public Defender's Office. As for the firm itself, Miss Lewis, was left holding the bag, and she'd be under investigation, with both, the Bar Association and the State of Illinois. It's questionable, rather, she'll be able to practice law, ever again.

Mr. TJ, had no family to come forward, to recover his remains. He too, was cremated at the expense of taxpayers.

All the girls involved, were recovering from their injuries, and were deported back, to their families. I only pray, that the cycle doesn't repeat for them.

Jimbo and his family, were free to go back and live a normal life. He left the trucking business, at the request of his wife, and now works a regular 9-to-5 job. He's now, able to go home every night.

Terri is enjoying her second chance at life, with her parents. In addition to that, she's studying for her GED, and plans on becoming a Social Worker.

Mr. Rafael Petreas, met his demise at the hands of the Cartel. When you live by the sword, you die by the sword!

Sally's became property of the state. Having been raided twice, it was closed and boarded up.

Linda McCoy continues, to make great strides in her law enforcement career. I get a real kick out of the Captain, keeping a close eye on her, all because of me!

Miss Candee Harris, got the counseling she needed, and returned to the W.L.O.K. News Crew. Now, she has respect for the people in uniform, who put their lives on the line, daily. It's still questionable, rather she will stay this way.

Councilman Lee, is still recovering from his injuries, but is planning to regain his reputation with the citizens of Chicago. We've spoken, but have no plans, of ever dating again.

The fact that I was involved in the death of the bikers, was never revealed to the public, or the top brass. As of today, it remains between me and the Captain. Finally, I stopped dreaming of a vacation, and went on a real one. This time, my timing was perfect. In another week, I'll be in good enough shape, to pack my things, climb onto my Sportster, and do something, I always wanted to do, head to Sturgis, for the Annual Harley-Davidson Rally.

The End.

ABOUT THE PUBLISHER

Let Life to Legacy bring your story to literary life! We offer the following publishing services: manuscript development, editing, transcription services, cover design, copyright services, ISBN assignment, worldwide distribution, and eBook conversion.

We make the publishing process easy. Throughout production, we keep the author informed every step of the way. Whether print-on-demand or trade publishing, we have packages to meet your publishing needs. At Life to Legacy, we take the stress out of becoming a published author.

Unlike other so-called publishers, we do more than just print books. Our books and eBooks are distributed to book buyers, distributors, and online retailers throughout the world. This is real publishing! Call us today for a free quote.

Please visit our website

www.Life2Legacy.com

or call us

708-272-4444

Send email inquiries to:

Life2Legacybooks@att.net

www.ingramcontent.com/pod-product-compliance
Lightning Source LLC
Chambersburg PA
CBHW030522020726
47494CB00004B/1203